"You make a habit of telling people to go for the gusto,"

said Zack.

"So?" asked Sunny.

"So," Zack said patiently, "you're not practicing what you preach. We've got the beginnings of something very interesting going on between us. Yet you don't seem willing to stick around to see how things will work out. In fact, I'm getting the impression that the idea scares you to death."

"That's not true," Sunny said automatically, but her head was spinning. Zack wasn't wasting any time on preliminaries . . . but then again, they didn't have much time.

"Really?" His low voice interrupted her thoughts. "Then prove it. Stick around, Sunny. At least stay for the fireworks."

Dear Reader,

Welcome to Silhouette—experience the magic of the wonderful world where two people fall in love. Meet heroines that will make you cheer for their happiness, and heroes (be they the boy next door or a handsome, mysterious stranger) who will win your heart. Silhouette Romance reflects the magic of love—sweeping you away with books that will make you laugh and cry, heartwarming, poignant stories that will move you time and time again.

In the coming months we're publishing romances by many of your all-time favorites, such as Diana Palmer, Brittany Young, Sondra Stanford and Annette Broadrick. Your response to these authors and our other Silhouette Romance authors has served as a touchstone for us, and we're pleased to bring you more books with Silhouette's distinctive medley of charm, wit and—above all—*romance*.

I hope you enjoy this book and the many stories to come. Experience the magic!

Sincerely,

Tara Hughes
Senior Editor
Silhouette Books

MELODIE ADAMS

The Medicine Man

Silhouette *Romance*

Published by Silhouette Books New York

America's Publisher of Contemporary Romance

For my mother, Diane,
who is also my very good friend.
Thanks for being there. And for being you.
My hope is that I will be as good a mother as you
have always been. This book is for you, Mom.
With much love.

Melodie

SILHOUETTE BOOKS
300 E. 42nd St., New York, N.Y. 10017

Copyright © 1989 by Melodie Adams

ISBN: 0-373-08647-4

First Silhouette Books printing May 1989

Printed in the U.S.A.

Silhouette Romance

I'll Fly the Flags #265
A Dangerous Proposition #516
The Medicine Man #647

Silhouette Special Edition

Gentle Possession #152

MELODIE ADAMS

spent her childhood years in various states west of the Mississippi and claims that it was "a terrific, ever-changing, always interesting way to grow up." Still, in spite of all the wonderful places she's seen, Melodie's favorite way to relax is to spend a day in the sun, a tall glass of iced tea in one hand and a good romance in the other.

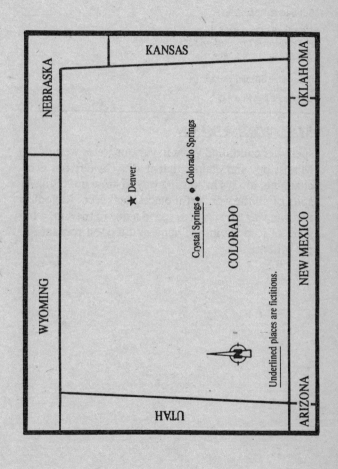

Chapter One

Out of the corner of her eye, she noticed him, but Sunny Eden deliberately avoided looking in his direction. He was trouble, she knew from experience. Already she could spot the hard-core doubters a mile away. But she also knew that this cynical, suspicious-looking man presented a challenge. And a challenge always made the blood run more quickly through her veins.

Unconsciously she straightened her shoulders and half-turned to pick up the small microphone. A smile tugging strongly at the corners of her mouth, she tossed her head a little to send the glistening gold of her shoulder-length hair away from her face. Her green eyes shimmered with a mixture of defiance and amusement as she met the dark-haired man's gaze and held it for the span of a few hard-hitting seconds. Then she gave her attention to her work.

Quickly, she scanned the immediate area for prospects. It was early yet, and the carnival midway of the small county fairground was not overly populated. This fact did not discourage Sunny. She often did her best business when the crowds were fairly small and there was not too much action along the midway to provide competition. It was during times like this that she could grab the most attention, and hold it long enough to make a sale.

With the mike in one hand, she reached with the other for her top hat, a red-and-white-striped version that matched the pinstripes of her 1890s-style three-piece suit. She placed the hat on her head and tapped it soundly on its top. Then she began.

Two middle-aged couples strolled in front of her booth, casting curious glances at the display behind her and the long table in front of her. Sunny donned a smile that was both boldly friendly and slightly conspiratorial. With an outstretched arm, she motioned for the foursome to come closer. Automatically, the people smiled and began to shake their heads, accustomed to being summoned by every professional barker along the midway. But like the professionals, Sunny Eden tried to avoid taking no for an answer.

She raised the microphone. "Come on folks, step right on over here and talk to me for a minute," she insisted. Courtesy made the two couples hesitate, and Sunny quickly pressed the advantage. "I've traveled all the way from Los Angeles, California, to let all you nice folks in the beautiful state of Colorado in on a little secret of mine. No, actually, it's a big secret," she promised, nodding earnestly at the foursome. "But I can't tell you about it if you're standing clear over there. Come a little closer, and I'll tell you all about the Garden of Eden..."

Without breaking eye contact, Sunny waved a hand to indicate the booth behind her. The red-painted metal trailer had doors that opened out from the side to provide a display of her goods, more of which were stored inside. Dr. Eden's Traveling Garden was lettered in gold.

"Step right up, folks, don't be shy! My name is Dr. Sunny Eden, and I'm here today to tell you that there's news—good news—about curing the modern-day afflictions that ail you. Are you worn out, strung out, tense or tired? Do you need to be picked up, perked up or maybe even calmed down? Are you overweight, underweight or just plain average? Does your hair and skin lack the luster of your youth? Is it hard to get around the way you once did? Is life passing you by because you haven't the energy or desire to keep up anymore?

"My friends, I am here today to tell you that things can change. From this moment on, you can be a new person—I *guarantee* it. Right here, in my Garden of

Eden, you can find the fountain of youth! I said, you can *find* the *fountain* of *youth*! Do I hear a 'hallelujah' for an announcement like that?''

Sunny lifted her eyebrows and looked at the small crowd that had formed during her speech with stern expectancy. There were a few nervous chuckles, but no hallelujahs. Long practice kept Sunny from smiling at this point, even though she always wanted to when she saw people trying to decide whether she was serious about her products, putting them on or simply a fruitcake left over from one of the old-time traveling medicine shows. Frowning, she narrowed her green eyes and cupped a hand near her ear.

"Say 'hallelujah,'" she demanded, stomping a foot. Then she whipped out a rolled sheet of paper from the pocket of her jacket and held the paper out in front of her for the audience to see.

"It's right here, in the script," she said, pointing a finger at the middle of the typed page. "'The crowd says 'hallelujah'! That's what it says, right after I tell you about the fountain of youth. Now, are you all going to do your part or not?''

As always, the audience began to relax, certain now that they were seeing an act rather than a mental case.

"Hallelujah! The fountain of youth!" One young man started the refrain, then others followed, laughing self-consciously.

"That's better." Sunny nodded and smiled in smug satisfaction as she rerolled the "script." "Now, where was I?" She pretended to search her memory while she waited for the full attention of her audience. What she had to say next was important. The audience already liked her. Now she gradually had to begin to make them take her seriously. That was always the tricky part....

"You were about to get yourself arrested for making fraudulent claims and practicing medicine without a license, that's where you were." The statement came from the dark-haired man standing on the fringe of the crowd—the man Sunny had spotted before she began.

The disbelief and contempt in his voice didn't surprise Sunny, since she'd had the same type of heckler before. But she always found it irritating when people were too narrow-minded to hear her out. Granted, her attention-getting spiel was a bit extravagant, but surely it was obvious that it was all in good fun—the grandiloquent words served mostly as an icebreaker so the audience would be more receptive to her message. After all, it was difficult to make vitamins sound exciting. Somehow she had to compete with all the other attractions along the midway; it wasn't an easy job.

Putting a hand to her forehead, Sunny shielded her eyes from the sun's glare and looked at the man. "Arrested?" she echoed, properly shocked, her mind searching for a way to ease back into her presentation. The man was stealing her thunder, and she didn't like it.

"For what? Certainly not for the reasons you stated. Fraudulent claims?" She removed her hand from her forehead and pressed it to her breastbone, as if taken aback by his accusations. "Sir, I assure you, there is nothing fraudulent in what I said. Behind me is the literature to prove it."

She gestured behind her at the stacks of pamphlets, that she passed out free, and of which she was as well-stocked as she was with vitamins and herbs and teas and natural cosmetics and beauty aids.

"And, beyond that," she said, "I myself am living proof that the fountain of youth is a real and reachable thing." She nodded sagely, her expression totally serious as she let her eyes scan the crowd. "I can see doubt in some of your expressions," she scolded. "But that doubt is misplaced. How old do all of you think I am?"

"Twenty-five!" someone shouted.

"Twenty-seven!"

"Eighteen!" This last guess came from a gangly young man who seemed hopeful that Sunny might be in his own age bracket.

Sunny shook her head. Actually she was twenty-eight, but that wasn't something she was telling.

"Well," she said smugly. "I can see that there's no point in letting you guess, so I'll just have to tell you. I had a birthday last week. On Tuesday, I turned ninety-three."

There were chuckles and giggles over this, and Sunny felt the tension the heckler had brought on dissipate. His seriousness now seemed churlish and out of place in this carnival atmosphere of fun and entertainment. But when she returned her gaze to the man, he was not laughing. Behind her own smile, Sunny ground her teeth. Obviously the man had no sense of humor. What in the world was he doing at the fair in the first place?

He stood for a moment, holding her gaze, sizing her up. He was a good-looking man, with tanned skin, a lean, fit body and chiseled features. He wore a red polo shirt and gray summer-weight slacks. Normally Sunny would have found him exceptionally attractive.

But, she thought a bit wistfully, beauty is as beauty does, and the man's intolerance and general attitude were decidedly ugly.

Lifting her chin, Sunny forced her gaze back to the rest of the group and hoped the grumpy man would hold his silence. Out of the corner of her eye, she spotted him moving and hoped he was leaving. The crowd was not on his side.

She went on with her speech, ignoring the man. Her eyes widened in surprise and dismay when the closest people parted and the man stepped up directly in front of her.

"I hate to interrupt," he said, "but I'm in a rush, and I've got some business with you before I leave."

"Business?" Sunny frowned at him blankly. Irritation bristled through her at his rude interruption. The crowd watched the exchange with a mixture of curiosity and discomfort.

"Yes." He plopped a brown paper sack atop her table with a heavy thud. "I have some merchandise I'd like to return."

"You have?" Sunny frowned doubtfully.

She was positive she'd never sold anything to him. He was abrasive and rude and had no sense of humor, but he really was also incredibly good-looking. Especially up close. His eyes were dark and glistening, framed by spiky black lashes, and his teeth, white and even, would have looked great if the man ever smiled. No, Sunny thought again, he definitely wasn't the type she would have forgotten.

But she had a crowd standing around, and she wasn't going to argue with the man in front of them. "Well," she said with a forced smile, "I'll be more than happy to discuss it with you in just a few minutes. If you wouldn't mind—"

"I would mind," he stated blandly. "Very much. I have an important appointment across town and not much time to get there. So..."

Sunny's lips tightened. This was her show, and he was ruining it. By the time she got through taking care of his problem, her audience would have lost interest—or faith. Obviously, he wasn't happy with whatever merchandise he'd gotten hold of. So why should anyone else buy it?

"So..." Sunny echoed sweetly. "Maybe you could stop back later on, when you'll have more time."

The man's black gaze ran over her, hardening to meet the challenge. Without another word, he opened the sack and began setting out bottle after bottle of vitamins. The merchandise was indeed hers. At a loss as to how to handle the situation, Sunny stared at the bottles.

"Well?" the man prompted, wadding up the now-empty sack. "You don't have any problem with refunding a customer's money, do you?" The question seemed louder than necessary to Sunny. It was a mixture of a threat and a demand.

"Why, no—not at all," she said quickly, flashing a smile around the group of people. "The Garden of Eden always aims to please." She hesitated, eyeing the merchandise with dismay. There was nearly a hundred dollars' worth. "May I ask the reason for this apparent change of heart?"

It was a tentative question, because she wasn't at all sure she wanted this man to offer any information, not with a group of spectators hanging around. But the man's obnoxious actions had already shredded any enthusiasm she might have drummed up. At least if he voiced his complaints, she might be able to answer them and save a few customers.

"Certainly," the man said. "I'm a doctor, and these—these pills of yours were bought by one of my patients. She showed them to me, and I immediately advised her against taking any of them. In my professional opinion they are worthless and could be dangerous. I came to return them myself to make sure that my patient, a sixty-two-year-old woman who would dearly love to find the 'fountain of youth,' would not be further coerced or swindled."

"I see." Sunny closed her eyes, knowing she was doomed. There wasn't a thing in the world she could say at this point to turn the tables and regain the trust and favor of the crowd. People began to drift off, for which she was grateful. All she wanted was to get the wretched man taken care of and out of the vicinity. She had known instinctively that he was dangerous, but not to this degree. Her blood boiled at the false impression he'd given—and her total inability to do anything about it. In the eyes of the general public, doctors were gods, never to be questioned. Sunny hated that unearned sort of blind loyalty.

Managing a tight smile, she reached under the table and pulled out her calculator. "I'm sorry you feel that way," she said tightly, concentrating on tapping out the prices on each of the bottles. "My only experience with any of the merchandise has been beneficial. I have scientific documentation to substantiate any claims I've made—"

"Including the fact that you're ninety-three, I suppose," the doctor said, sarcasm threading his voice.

Sunny looked up sharply. The man's face was impassive. Everyone else had moved on, their interest in the Garden of Eden lost for good. Aware that they were alone, Sunny saw no more need for false politeness or attempts at keeping her temper in check.

"You know something, mister—"

"Doctor," he stressed.

Sunny chose to ignore it. "Whatever," she snapped. "You have absolutely no sense of humor at all."

"Not where the health of my patients is concerned, no," he said smoothly. "I take that very seriously, and you should, too, Miss E—"

"*Doctor* Eden," Sunny interrupted.

"You aren't a doctor." His voice derided the mere suggestion of such a thing.

Sunny studied him for a few silent seconds, then lifted her chin a fraction of an inch. "That is my professional name, and I am, at this moment, on the job. Of course, I also have a PhD in nutrition, but that's not why I use the title. I chose it, Doctor, not in an attempt to validate myself, or to fool and swindle the public, but because I thought it was amusing, in the spirit of the old-time medicine shows—as befitted a carnival booth and show. Obviously, since you seem to have no sense of humor or of nostalgia or of old-fashioned showmanship, I couldn't possibly expect you to understand what I've tried to do here—"

"What I understand," he said, "is that you are a health hazard. Lady, whether you realize it or not, you are dangerous. Doesn't that fact bother you at all?"

Sunny crossed her arms and glared at him. "It would, if it were true. What exactly is it that you have against health foods, mister? Afraid you might lose a few customers? I should think you'd be glad if your patients are becoming more health conscious—"

"Health conscious? My mother spent more than two hundred dollars on this junk yesterday—and none of it is going to change the fact that she's sixty-two years old. She came home with her head filled with crazy notions about fat-burning pills and vitamins to restore the natural color of her hair and some tonic to drink to cure arthritis, and I don't know what all else— Oh, yes." He snapped his fingers. "She had a bag of—things—little seeds or something—that she plans to grow in her kitchen. Some grass that she's going to run through the juicer and drink! After talking to you, she thinks drinking grass juice is going to have all kinds of miraculous effects."

"For your obviously limited information, *Doctor*, wheatgrass therapy has been successful as a general health builder and disease fighter. It's the chlorophyll." Turning her back to him, Sunny plucked the relevant pamphlets from her display and faced the doctor, armed. "This—" she slapped a bottle of capsules and the related pamphlet down on the table in front of him "—is a growth hormone, which has been useful in burning stored fat *and* building new muscle. As for this—" another bottle, another pamphlet "—studies indicate that restoration of natural hair color could be influenced by a combination of the two active ingredients. And, finally, the arthritis. Carrot juice has, in some cases, been effective in treating arthritis sufferers. It's all here, Doctor. I didn't write any of it."

He opened his mouth, then closed it stubbornly, appearing to change his mind about whatever he'd been going to say. He shook his head and blew out a long, exasperated breath. "I'm not going to argue with you. You people are a waste of time."

Sunny's eyes narrowed. "So are you people. I am continually amazed at the medical profession. Progress is being made, and you absolutely refuse to recognize it, calling it quackery. But if people are being helped, why on earth can't you—"

He held up a silencing hand. "Forget it, *Doctor*. Your so-called proof is too flimsy, and I've heard all the unfounded arguments before. Just give me my mother's money, and I'll leave you to your quackery."

"Fine," Sunny said evenly, knowing he was right. There was absolutely no point in pursuing the discussion. He was absolutely set in his opinions—like too many other people. If something was new or different or even slightly unorthodox, it had to be wrong. Few things infuriated Sunny Eden, but this archaic, harmful attitude always did the trick.

Tight-lipped, she totaled the prices with the calculator and counted out the man's refund. Before she gave it to him, she made a project out of checking the seal on every bottle of vitamins.

"Nothing's been opened," he growled. "Take my word for it."

"I wouldn't take your word for anything, Doctor," Sunny informed him. "I make a habit of getting my information from reliable sources." Satisfied that the bottles hadn't been tampered with, she ignored his outstretched hand and put the money on the table. "There you go," she said. "I hope your mother spends it in good health, although with an advisor like you around, I doubt that that's possible." She started to turn away, then hesitated, his accusations nagging at her. "Just for the record, Doctor, what did your mother buy from me that you consider so dangerous?"

For a split-second he seemed off guard. Then a humorless half-smile slanted his mouth. "Mostly, I guess it was your line, Doctor. She bought every word you said. And when a sixty-two-year-old woman thinks she's found the fountain of youth, that can be dangerous. What do you think would happen if she took all this worthless junk and found out you were wrong?"

"But she wouldn't!" Sunny protested. "With the right diet, moderate exercise and the right supplements, she *would* feel younger, more energetic, more—"

He stuffed the money into his slacks pocket. "The only thing I can guarantee is that she'd feel more broke. She still has about a hundred bucks worth of stuff at home—stuff she'd opened before I got home last night. She'd already started jars full of bean sprouts, and she's got pans full of dirt all over the kitchen—her grass is planted, and I've been ordered not to touch it." He shook his head. "It wasn't a total loss for you, Dr. Eden, so you ought to feel grateful that I didn't get home a few hours earlier. But I do want to warn you: if my mother comes back out here and you sell her anything, I'm bringing it back."

"Against her wishes," Sunny stated scornfully.

"Yep." He grinned. "So be forewarned—if you sell to Martha Granger, don't spend the money."

Martha, Sunny thought. Oh, not Martha! She had talked with and advised the woman for nearly half an hour the previous day. They had hit it off immediately.

"How am I supposed to know your mother?" she said. "I don't ask my customers their names. I guess you'll have to tell her to announce herself and remind me not to let her buy anything."

He shrugged. "I don't think she'll be back anyway. She's had since last night to think about what I told her. I'm sure she's probably come to her senses by now. You really cast some spell over her." He shook his head. "After watching you manipulate that crowd, I can see why my mother was so taken in."

Sunny stared at him coldly. "I thought you had an appointment, Doctor. You're going to be late."

"I've got plenty of time. I had to say something to keep you from selling to that crowd. You know you had them eating out of your hand."

"Almost." Sunny didn't deny it. "That's my job, Doctor. To interest and persuade. I do it very well because I believe in my products and principles. There will be another crowd, I assure you. Your childish attempt at ruining my business was futile. I've got what people are looking for—some of the answers they need and are not getting from so-called health professionals like you. I'll always have customers, Doctor. But with any luck, people like me will eventually be able to put people like you out of business. That's my goal, and I'm proud of it."

Half-smiling, he shook his head. "For some reason, I'm not too worried for my job. Of course, I'm not too positive about yours."

"You don't have to be," she said stiffly. "Because I am."

"Which is why you travel with a carnival—keep on the move so you'll have new suckers every week, new little old ladies to swindle..."

"Doctor, you are on my time. If you'd like to continue this discussion, you can pay for it. Otherwise, I'm going to have to ask you to leave me to my work. There is such a thing as harassment, and you've entered into that territory. Keep it up, and you may find me parked in your office, telling your patients the same kinds of lies that you have just used to run off my customers." His smile began to widen, and Sunny went on coldly, "If you doubt that I'll do it, just hang around."

His dark eyes narrowed. "I don't doubt for a minute that you'd do it, whether it could be potentially harmful to a patient or not. You'd do it anyway, just for the principle of the thing. That's what scares me about people like you."

Sunny held his gaze. "Funny, Doctor. That's the very same thing that scares me about people like you. Now, if you'll excuse me, the crowd is picking up, and I'm going to have to work twice as hard to make up for the damage you've done. If you want to avoid retaliation, at your patients' expense, I suggest you be on your way." She began straightening the table display, sorting the bottles he'd returned and putting them in their correct order.

"Just one more question, Doctor," he said sarcastically. "Do you get many customers like my mother?"

"You mean older people?"

"No, I mean people willing to spend hundreds of dollars for this worthless junk."

Sunny smiled. "All the time. You know what they say, Doctor: one man's junk is another man's treasure. And as you well know, the cost of health care is extremely high. How much do you charge for an office visit?"

"None of your business," he said smoothly. "You can't even begin to compare a medical office with this—this sideshow you're running."

"No, you're absolutely right. My show and advice is free. If people want to hear you talk, they've got to pay through the nose. That really makes me wonder, Doctor, which one of us is the real con artist."

"Stop wondering." With a disgusted look, he turned and started to walk away.

"Don't worry, Doctor, I already have. I stopped wondering about that a long time ago...." She sat for a minute, watching him leave. "Three years ago," she murmured to herself. Her shoulders slumped a little under the weight of her memories. "If only" was a phrase she'd tried to wipe out of her vocabulary, but there were times when it came back to haunt her. Now was one of those times, and she resented Dr. Granger for his part in stirring up the past.

But then again, she thought, maybe it was good. Remembering always freshened her vision of what she was really trying to accomplish—and the importance of it all. So maybe she should thank Dr. Granger for reminding her. Slipping off her stool, she put the top hat back on her head and patted its crown. She reached for the microphone.

"Step right on up here, folks. Now, don't be shy, I've come all the way from Los Angeles, California, to let you all in on a little secret. No, actually, it's a big secret..."

The secret that there were options, alternatives. And if the doctors of this country weren't going to tell anyone about them, Sunny Eden was.

Chapter Two

Dr. Zachary Granger fumed all the way home. Dr. Sunny Eden was one of the nerviest women he had ever met in his life. Calling *him* dangerous! Good grief, the woman actually believed all that garbage put out by the vitamin companies. Didn't she know that if all that tripe were true, most of the population would be glowing with health?

But, of course, Zack realized with a wry smile, that was exactly what she'd been trying to tell him. But he hadn't attended years and years of school to have some sideshow quack tell him anything about physical health.

Shaking his head, he tried to put Dr. Eden out of his mind. He had a whole day off today, the first in quite a while, and he intended to enjoy what remained of it. Maybe he'd shoot a leisurely eighteen out at the club this afternoon. It was a beautiful day for it—warm but not hot, with a light, fresh, mountain breeze. Zack thought that summer in the Crystal Springs area of Colorado must be one of the most pleasant settings in the world.

He turned the car into the driveway and walked up to the house. It was a white, two-story clapboard, and he'd lived there since birth. He loved the old, cozily elegant place. When he'd set up his practice, he'd debated whether to hang a shingle in one of the medical buildings in town or to do as his father had done and use part of the house. He had decided to follow tradition and reopen his dad's old office. It had a separate entrance, and the arrangement worked out very well. Also, he thought his mother liked having him so close. She'd been lonely since Zack's father had died, and Zack did his best to ease some of that.

Key in hand, he first tried the knob on the front door. Unlocked. He frowned. How many times had he warned his mother about leaving the house open when she was home alone? The woman was too trusting, just as she had proven once again with that Eden woman. Zack was just glad he was around to protect her. Times had changed, but Martha Granger couldn't seem to see that fact.

"Ma, I'm home!" Zack announced, absently jingling his keys.

There was no response, but he could hear the portable television set in the kitchen. Martha liked her daytime soaps, and he had probably walked in at a particularly suspenseful moment.

But when he walked through the doorway, his mother wasn't even looking at the TV. She was standing in front of the sink, staring out the window. Her arms were folded over her ribs, and her mouth looked tight, lips pursed. She was obviously lost in thought and didn't even seem to know that Zack was in the house. He sighed. Apparently her hearing was beginning to go, too.

"Hi, Ma," he said, and kissed her cheek. "You look like you're a million miles away."

She turned to face him, but there was no change in her expression. "Right now, I'd like to be about a million miles away."

Zack frowned. "What's wrong?" He glanced out the window, wondering if something outside had upset her. Everything looked fine to him. "Did you get some bad news today or something?"

"Yes," Martha Granger said tightly. "As a matter of fact, I did." Uncrossing her arms, she walked past him and poured herself a cup of coffee. She didn't think to offer him one, and Zack's frown deepened. He didn't think he could ever remember his mother forgetting her manners. Especially when it came to him. He was an only child, and both his parents had doted on him. He didn't feel that he had been spoiled, but he knew he had been much-loved, a feeling that he had always reciprocated in full.

He watched his mother sit down at the table. "Well? What's the news?"

Her lips tightened again, and then she finally looked straight at him. "The news," she said, "is that I've raised a tyrant for a son."

Zack blinked. "What?" He pulled out a chair and sat down across from her. "What are you talking about?"

Her gray eyes blazed. Zack had to stifle the urge to squirm. He hadn't been the recipient of that look for many years, but he remembered it well. It was the same look she'd had when he'd gotten suspended from high school for cutting class and for the time when—

"I'm talking about the way you've been taking it upon yourself to run my life these days," his mother said. "This may come as news to you, young man, but I am perfectly capable of making my own decisions. I was taking care of this house and your father and running the office and paying the bills and doing charity work and a hundred other things before you were even born. And you know something? I don't care how many years of schooling you've had. I still know more than you do, and as long as I'm alive, I always will! And do you know why? Because I've lived longer, that's why!" She pushed herself to her feet. "And one of the things that I will always know more about than you do is how I want to run my life. And from now on, that's just exactly what I intend to do! Any questions?''

Her look dared him to say a word. Zack knew he was nearly gaping at her, but he couldn't help himself. This was not his mother. Good Lord, he hoped senility wasn't setting in, but an unprovoked outburst like this was not a good sign. He stood up and peered at her in concern.

''Mom, do you feel okay?'' It was a cautious question. Heaven only knew what might set her off again.

''I feel just fine,'' she said evenly, and there was a new glint in her gray eyes. ''As a matter of fact, I feel better than I've felt in about six years.''

Six years. It had been six years since his father had died. Zack's eyes widened. Six years next week. His mother always got very morose on the anniversary of Doc Granger's death. Perhaps all this had something to do with that.

''Mom, I think you should sit down. It isn't good for you to get yourself all worked up like this—'' He tried to take her arm, but she knocked his hand aside.

''Just stop it, Zack,'' she commanded. ''I'm not having any more of this—this overprotective pampering. Now, I'll admit that it hasn't all been your fault. After Doc died, I pretty well fell apart. And I did lean on you a lot, and I guess this whole crazy situation just became a habit. But it's time for a change. I have a life to live, and I'm going to live it. Just as you need to start living yours.''

"Living mine? I do live my life. I like my life. And I guess I must be dense or something, because I do not understand what's so awful about yours. What is it you're wanting to do that you're not doing now?"

"*Live*, Zack. Don't you know what that means? It means enjoying life instead of just going through it. It means feeling good and looking good and taking some chances." A wry smile curved her lips. "It means going for the gusto, kid, and it's high time I started doing that again."

Zack frowned. *Going for the gusto, kid?* This really was not his mother. Oh, no, not at all. He couldn't begin to imagine what had brought all this on... Unless...

"Wait a minute," he murmured, eyes suddenly narrowing. "Does all this have anything to do with that fruitcake woman out at the fairgrounds?"

Martha Granger stiffened. "I don't happen to think that Sunny Eden is a fruitcake. I do think, however, that she is a lovely young woman with a lot of lovely ideas about life." Her look became speculative. "I also think that if you could manage to find yourself a woman like her, you'd be a much happier man."

Zack stared. "Mom! That woman is a borderline psychotic, not to mention a major health hazard!" He put his hands on his hips. "I thought we had all this settled last night. We discussed all of her products and sales pitches and nonsense, and we agreed that she's

nothing but a con artist—a very dangerous con artist."

Martha looked down, and her fingers began fid-
dling with the collar of her floral-print blouse. Zack
stifled a small sigh of relief. The angry rebelliousness
was beginning to fade, and his real, sensible mother
showed signs of returning.

"Well, now that's true," Martha admitted. "We did
discuss it, and, at the time, a lot of what you said
made sense."

Zack raised an eyebrow. *At the time?*

"But," his mother continued, "I never really agreed
that you could take my vitamins back—"

"But you said—"

"I didn't say much of anything, if you'll recall."
She straightened her shoulders. "You did most of the
talking, and I did most of the listening. For a while I
was nearly convinced that you might be right. After
all, you are a doctor. But then I got to thinking. There
is a lot a value in supplements and herbs and such.
Years ago, even your father would prescribe herb teas
and that kind of thing when it seemed appropriate.
And my old granny used to mix all kinds of potions
for our family—and they worked, too. Not for everything, of course, but they did seem to work."

She sighed, pausing for a second. "With all the ad-
vertising that pharmaceutical companies do, plus their
sponsorship of medical schools, it's no wonder we've
gotten away from the natural ways of doing things. A

hundred times a day we're told to take a pill for this and take a pill for that. And you doctors—you're hardly taught anything in med school about nutrition and prevention. You're taught about drugs and surgeries, which is fine in its place. But all that should be a last resort. First and foremost, we should take care of ourselves—"

"*I* know that," Zack stated incredulously. "And if you recall, Mother, I am after you twenty-four hours a day to take care of yourself."

Martha grinned wryly. "Twenty-eight hours a day, but who's counting?" She sat back down at the table. "At any rate, I've decided it's high time that I started taking responsibility for myself again, and that includes deciding what I put into my body. I like the things I bought from Sunny Eden yesterday, and I am going to use them." She shot him a warning glance. "Maybe they won't do me any good, I don't know. But I don't believe for a minute that they're going to hurt me."

"They could," Zack protested. "Certain supplements in high dosages can—"

"Yes," she agreed. "They can be dangerous if not taken in the right amounts—like aspirin or any other drug. I'm not a fool, Zack, and I'd appreciate not being treated like one."

"I'm sorry. I didn't think I was treating you like one."

"Well," she said gently, "it wasn't all your fault. As I said, I allowed this situation to develop by becoming so dependent on you. However, I never did tell you that you could return the things I bought from Miss Eden."

"But I thought—"

"I know. You thought I'd go along with whatever you decided. That's been the pattern lately, and I apologize for letting it happen. From now on, I want you to worry about yourself, all right? Concentrate on finding out what it takes to make *you* happy. And, son?"

"Yes, Mother?" he answered warily.

"If you really want to worry about my happiness, why don't you start thinking about giving me some grandchildren."

With that, Martha Granger got up, put her coffee cup in the sink and left the kitchen. A little dazed, Zack stared after her. He could hear his mother humming cheerfully as she climbed the stairs to her room.

Whaaack! The ball flew straight down the middle of the fairway.

"Hey, Granger, what'd you do? Eat your Wheaties this morning?"

Zack forced a smile and plunked his driver back in the golf bag. "Just luck, boys," he said to the other three men who made up today's foursome. "Just luck."

He climbed into the driver's side of the golf cart and punched the gas pedal to the floor. His passenger, Bob Fielding, grabbed the edge of the cart to keep from being jolted out. "What's with you today, Zack?" Bob asked. "I'll admit you're shooting some darned good golf, but your company leaves a lot to be desired."

"Sorry. I've just got a lot on my mind." Zack braked to a halt next to Bob's ball. The other two men were off to the left, searching the woods for Stan Bernstein's ball.

As a rule, none of the four doctors were exceptional golfers, but they enjoyed the game and the chance to get out of the office during the week, and that was good enough. Today Zack was shooting close to par, and under normal circumstances he would have been thrilled. But nothing about this day had been normal, and he was having a hard time taking any satisfaction at all in his game.

He still couldn't believe this morning's conversation with his mother. All this upheaval, and one person to blame—Ms. Sunny Eden. Just thinking about the woman made Zack want to grind his teeth, hence the energy in his golf swing.

"Anything I can help with, pal?" Bob asked, pushing his glasses up.

Bob Fielding was a plastic surgeon and a friend of Zack's since kindergarten. But somehow Zack couldn't bring himself to tell him about his mother or

Sunny Eden. He supposed it was a problem that would resolve itself in time. His mother had been the victim of a pro's sales pitch and pep talk, and it would take a few days or so for it to wear off. Plus, the carnival would be leaving in another week, taking Dr. Sunny Eden along with it. After that, everything would get back to normal, he was sure.

"No, thanks, Bob. It's just been one of those days. Now, why don't you get out there and take a swing at that ball and see if you can provide me with a little competition here. In case you haven't noticed, son, I'm hot today."

In more ways than one, Zack thought, but he felt himself beginning to relax. The more he thought about it, the more he was positive that his mother was just going through a phase and had needed to blow off a little steam. In fact, by the time he got home for dinner, his mother would probably be back to her old self, buzzing happily around the kitchen as she fixed their usual Wednesday night fare—baked breaded pork chops, fried potatoes and onions, applesauce and green beans.

Zack smiled to himself and turned his attention to his game.

"Martha!" Sunny looked up at the woman in surprise. "What are you doing here? I thought—" Automatically she glanced around, looking for Martha Granger's obnoxious offspring.

"I came to apologize for my son," the older woman said. "Sometimes he can be a little...overbearing."

A little, Sunny thought wryly. "That's okay, Martha. I'm just sorry he feels the way he does about what I'm doing here. I really believe in my merchandise, or I wouldn't be selling it."

"Oh, I believe in it, too," Martha hurried to assure her. "That's the other reason I'm here—to buy back the things he returned this morning." She opened her purse and took out her wallet.

"Oh!" Sunny blinked in surprise. "I see." She licked her lips. "Uh, Martha, does Dr. Granger know you're here?"

While she was thrilled that Martha was more open-minded than her son, she wasn't exactly anxious to have a repeat of this morning's performance. The whole spectacle had been highly humiliating.

"No." Martha shook her gray head. "He doesn't know I'm here. In fact, he'll probably have an absolute fit when he finds out I came back. Now, let's see, what did I have before? Some of this..." She picked up a brown bottle.

"Uh, Martha, are you sure you want to do this? I mean, apparently it's causing a lot of problems between you and your son." And apparently, the son totally ignored his mother's wishes. Which meant if she kept buying the stuff, he would probably keep bringing it back, just as he had threatened. "Maybe you should try to resolve this thing before you buy any more.''

"Oh, no, dear." Martha waved a dismissing hand. "It's resolved. I had a long talk with him this morning, and I don't think he'll dare to say another word on the subject." She grinned impishly, her gray eyes sparkling with mischief. "I guess you could say I laid down the law. I don't think we'll have to worry about him interfering again."

Sunny tipped her head to the side and smiled in wonder. This was not the same woman who had seemed so indecisive and shy the previous afternoon; this was a woman who had taken charge of her life.

"Good for you, Martha!" she exclaimed, genuinely excited for her. "I'm always thrilled to hear about people standing up for their rights. Sometimes it's a pretty tough thing to do." Especially if one had a son like the illustrious Dr. Granger.

Martha looked thoughtful. "It was pretty tough," she admitted. "And it caught Zachary completely by surprise. Actually, I'm afraid I was a little rough on him. I had spent all morning fuming about him bringing my things back, and by the time he got home I was ready—more than ready—to let him have it." She shook her head. "Of course, there was more to it than just the vitamins. I've been depending on him for nearly everything ever since my husband died. It was so much easier to let Zack do my thinking for me. But after listening to you yesterday, it reminded me of

what it was like to be young, to really live my life."
Her gaze became sober. "If it's not too late, I want to
try to do that again."

There was so much yearning in the statement that
Sunny's heart went out to the woman. "Martha," she
said gently, patting the woman's hand, "it's never too
late. You know that as well as I do. All you have to do
is make up your mind about what you want and go
after it. And don't let anybody stand in your way."

"Well, Miss Eden, that's my intention. But to tell
you the truth, I'm not exactly sure where to start. I
guess the first step is to buy back all the things that are
going to help me stay healthy. And after that . . ."

Sunny glanced at her watch. It was two o'clock, and
business was slow. And besides, trying to help people
feel better and enjoy a better quality of life was her
business—her business, and since Dan, her personal
life's goal. She chewed her lip for a second, then made
her decision.

"After that, Martha, why don't you and I spend the
afternoon at the fair? I'm due for a break, and I
haven't had lunch."

"Lunch?" Martha's face glowed with surprised
pleasure. "That would be lovely. And they do have
some interesting exhibits in the arts-and-crafts building."

"Exhibits?" Sunny raised an eyebrow. "I wasn't
talking about visiting exhibits, Martha. I'm talking

about living a little. The midway, kid. This carnival has got some wild rides...."

"You *what*?" Zack exploded, staring at his mother in disbelief. She had gone mad. Stark, raving mad.

"You heard me," Martha said pleasantly. She walked past him to the kitchen, a bag of groceries in one arm. Zack followed at her heels. "I rode the Zipper and the Wild Mouse and the Tilt-a-Whirl and the—"

"Mother!" He ran a hand through his black hair. "What in the h—"

"Zachary, you watch your language. I've never tolerated swearing in this house, and I never will. Now, you were saying?" She set the groceries on the counter.

Zack blew out a long breath and tried to calm himself. "I was saying, what in blue blazes were you thinking of, riding all those dangerous rides?"

"Dangerous?" Martha scoffed, and opened the refrigerator. "I hardly think they'd be allowed to run if they were dangerous, Zack. I had a marvelous time. More fun than I've had in years."

"They could be dangerous to you," Zack insisted with what he thought was the utmost patience. "Ma, you're sixty-two years old, for crying out loud. Your heart—"

"My heart," she said tightly, "is perfectly fine, as you well know. It's never given me a moment's trouble, and I'm certainly not expecting it to now."

"Mom, you can't be too careful at your age. You—"

"Oh, no, son," Martha said, shooting him a glance. "That's where you're wrong. You can be too careful, especially at my age. And I'm through doing that. Now, let's talk about something else, shall we? What would you like for dinner?"

"What would I like for dinner?" Zack frowned. "What do you mean, what would I like for dinner? It's Wednesday, isn't it? We always have pork chops and—"

"Well, we're not having pork chops tonight. For one thing, it would take too long to bake them. It's nearly six now. And for another thing, all that grease in the chops and fried potatoes isn't too good for us. And for another thing, I'm tired of having the same old thing on the same old night of the week, aren't you?"

Once again Zack was gaping at this stranger who called herself his mother. She hadn't been home fixing dinner when he'd returned from his golf game. She hadn't left a note. He'd been worried sick about her, and she'd come bouncing in as if nothing were wrong. She'd spent the afternoon at the fair riding the Zipper! And now she was changing a routine that had existed as long as he could remember. Zack didn't like this, not one little bit.

"No!" he said. "No, I'm not tired of it at all. Actually, I sort of like knowing what to plan on—what to look forward to."

"In that case," his mother said, "maybe you should take up cooking. Because if I'm doing the cooking, I plan on getting a little more adventurous from now on. The Rickshaw is offering some Oriental cooking lessons starting next week. I thought I might sign up— but we can talk about that later, too. Right now you're hungry, I know. So am I. Starved, actually." She dug into the grocery bag and pulled out a plastic bag of something white and cheesy-looking. "Maybe I'll do something with this tofu tonight. Sunny gave me this really interesting recipe for . . ."

Zack clenched his teeth and stopped listening to his mother. Sunny Eden again. One way or another he was going to bring all this nonsense to a halt.

It was midnight. The midway was shutting down for the day, and the few lingering fairgoers were slowly making their way toward the exits. Sunny sighed and leaned her folding chair back on its two hind legs. It had been a long day, but a satisfying one. The crowds had been good tonight, and she had moved a lot of merchandise. She had also met a very sweet, very shy, very insecure young girl named Cheryl.

In every town, in every crowd, there was always a Cheryl. Overweight, poor complexion, lank, styleless hair and absolutely no self-esteem. Knowing how painful adolescence could be, Sunny always made a point of trying to draw the Cheryls of this world into conversation and into her confidence. Sometimes all it took was a sympathetic ear and a little advice and the awkward little ducklings bloomed into swans.

And then, of course, there had been Martha. Sunny smiled, remembering the few hours she had spent with the lady. They had both had a wonderful time. And it had been so gratifying and heartwarming to watch the older woman shed the shackles she had allowed the years to place upon her. Yes, all in all, it had been quite a fulfilling day.

A fond smile still lingering on her lips, Sunny got up and began packing away her wares. She locked the trailer, gathered her purse and her cash box, turned to head home and found herself looking into a pair of dark eyes.

"Hello, Dr. Eden," Zachary Granger drawled. "Don't tell me the voodoo queen is putting away her pins and needles for the night? It's twelve o'clock—the witching hour. I'd have thought you'd be just getting started."

Sunny straightened her shoulders. "Hello, Dr. Granger. I'm surprised it took you so long to get here. Your mother left here hours ago. I would have expected you to hotfoot it over here as soon as you found out that she—" Sunny stopped suddenly as an amusing thought occurred to her. "Wait a minute," she murmured. "You didn't get here sooner because—"

She giggled. She couldn't help it. The thought of what this big, handsome, tough-guy type must have done tonight was hilarious.

"You didn't get here sooner because you had to wait for your mother to go to bed, didn't you? You were afraid that if you left, she'd know you were coming back here and she'd be furious."

A muscle in Zachary Granger's jaw leapt. "That is ridiculous." But it wasn't, and Zack knew it. He'd thought his mother would never turn off the blasted TV and go up to bed. But how in heaven's name had Sunny Eden known that? The woman really was a witch.

He felt a warm flush crawling up his cheeks, and knew he had to redirect the conversation. He was not here to discuss the disintegration of his relationship with his mother. He was here to discuss the dissipation of Sunny Eden's relationship with her. It had to come to a stop. It simply had to end, and it was going to end. Zack had no intention of allowing it to go on until the carnival left town.

Enough was enough and, as far as the Granger family was concerned, Dr. Sunny Eden was history.

Chapter Three

I waited until closing time because I wanted to be sure I had your undivided attention," Zack said scornfully.

"Oh." Sunny forced a sober expression, but amusement danced in her green eyes. "I see. This sounds very serious, Doctor."

"It is," Zack nearly growled, aware that she was making fun of him. How was he going to get through to this infuriating woman? He took a couple of steps closer to her and shoved his hands into the front pockets of his gray slacks. "I think you should know, Miss E—"

"*Doctor* Eden."

"Dr. Eden," he snapped, then hurried on before she could interrupt again. "I think you should know that what you encouraged my mother to do today was irresponsible and—"

"I quite agree, Dr. Granger."

Zack blinked in surprise. After his fruitless go-around with her this morning, he hadn't expected it to be this easy. "You do? You agree?"

"Yes." Sunny nodded. "I was thoroughly irresponsible. But perhaps that's because I'm not responsible."

Zack frowned. "What?"

She shrugged. "I'm not responsible for anything your mother says or does or thinks. She's a grown woman, Dr. Granger, and she's perfectly capable of thinking and acting for herself. Come to think of it, you're not responsible for her, either. I thought she made that plain to you this morning."

The flush was coming back again, bringing heat to his face. He couldn't believe that his mother had discussed him with this—this woman! He was losing ground and losing it fast. And he felt like a total, blundering fool.

"What does it take to get through to someone like you?" he asked. "You take a sixty-two-year-old woman on rides that could cause a heart attack, you swindle her out of hundreds of dollars for a bunch of worthless junk, you—"

Sunny sighed heavily and shook her head. There was no point in talking to the man. He was wasting her time. "Look, Doctor, it's been a long day. I am not going to defend my work to you anymore. You're a closed-minded dinosaur, and that's your problem. I just hope your mother doesn't go back to letting it be her problem. But either way, I'm calling it a day." She shifted the weight of the cash box to her other side. "Nightie-night, Doc. I need my beauty sleep a lot more than I need your hassles." Tossing her hair back, she headed down the midway.

"Hey!" Zack yelled. "I'm not through with you yet! Wait a minute!"

Sunny kept walking. Suddenly she felt very tired. She pressed her lips together and wished Zachary Granger hadn't shown up to inject such a sour note into her day. Everything had gone so well, and she'd felt so good about—

Strong fingers clamped themselves around her upper arm.

Stunned that he would have the nerve to grab her, Sunny stopped abruptly and turned on him. As her eyes met his, hot electricity seemed to crackle through the cool night air.

Behind him, the lights of the Ferris wheel danced and whirled, haloing his dark head with a multicolored glow. She became less conscious of the pressure of his fingers and more conscious of the heat they were producing. Her flesh felt as though it were on fire.

"You wanted something, Dr. Granger?" Her voice was supposed to sound icy, but there was a sudden huskiness in it that robbed it of most of its chill.

"I—" Zack paused and swallowed. What was the matter with him? His throat felt tight, and he felt hot all over. He had known enough women in his time to recognize physical attraction when it hit him, but this was ridiculous. This, he realized, was chemistry: pure, potent, biological chemistry, the likes of which had nothing to do with the mental processes or anything else...the likes of which he couldn't ever recall falling victim to before.

He was incredibly conscious of everything about her: the silky flow of her golden hair, the satin-smoothness of her creamy skin, the night-darkened depth of her green, green eyes...the light jasmine scent of her perfume and another, more subtle smell, the warm, clean scent of herself, wholly female and wholly inviting. All the anger that he had felt toward this woman was transformed into a different kind of energy—an energy that was much more powerful and basic.

"I...Sunny— Dr. Eden... Could we go someplace and talk about this? I mean, just...talk?"

Sunny swallowed. She couldn't seem to tear her gaze away from his dark, dark eyes. At close range, Zachary Granger was absolutely mesmerizing. Her nerve endings were sizzling, and the breath kept catching in her throat.

"Talk?" she echoed blankly.

He was so close, she could feel the moist warmth of his breath on her cheek. The only thing touching her was his hand, but his lean, hard body was only a few inches away. How long had it been since she'd allowed herself to feel the warmth of a man's arms? *Too long, Sunny,* a little voice whispered. *Much too long.*

"Yeah," Zack murmured. "Talk. No fighting, no arguing. Just...talk. Maybe we could come to some sort of...understanding."

"I suppose," Sunny said. "I suppose we could try it...."

His grip on her arm tightened a fraction. "Let's go." There was an urgency in his voice.

"Where to?"

"I don't know. A restaurant?" *Anyplace!* Zack wanted to say. *Anyplace that will give us a chance to get to know each other better. To get beyond all the issues that stand between us, so we can get on to the more important things....*

Sunny hesitated, knowing she was about to make a big mistake, but hoping against hope that somehow she might be wrong. "My place," she said, and turned away from the spell of his gaze and headed down the midway.

What have I done, what have I done? Sunny wailed in her mind. *I don't even like this man, and I'm taking him home with me!*

The lights of the fair were far behind them now as Sunny led the way to the fairground's camping area. Travel trailers and motor homes were scattered everywhere, most with lights burning in the windows. It would be an hour or two before most of the carnival people wound down and went to sleep. Sunny had the feeling that, tonight, sleep was going to elude her for a long, long time.

Walking beside her, Zack was silent and thoughtful, too. And tense. Sunny could feel it. She was fairly certain that he was experiencing the same second thoughts that she was having. This was a mistake. It was absolutely crazy. The only thing they had in common was a strong dislike for each other—and a strong physical thing for each other. But that wasn't justification, and they both knew it.

Yet neither one of them seemed to know how to set things back on their rightful course. On impulse, they had both crossed some intangible but very real line. Now the question was how to get back on the other side. The safe, sane side. The side that would leave them with a lot less to regret come morning.

They were nearing her camper. Sunny felt the panic mount. She knew that if she didn't act quickly, it would be too late. If he touched her... Well, if he touched her again, she wasn't altogether sure what her reaction would be.

Abruptly she stopped and faced him. "Dr. Granger..."

He stopped, too. This time they both were careful to keep a little distance between them. "Yes, Dr. Eden?"

Sunny cleared her throat. "You know, I've been thinking. It really is awfully late..."

"Yes," Zack said, seizing the coming excuse like a lifeline. Taking this any further would have been a major mistake, but he hated it that she was the first one to come to her senses. "Yes, it is...very late." But it was with a definite degree of regret that he helped put their plans to their early death. It was, of course, the right thing to do, but it was hardly the most satisfying.

"Perhaps we should...talk...another time," Sunny said, knowing it would never happen. It had been a moment of weakness, nothing more. A part of her was saddened by the realization.

"Yeah. Another time." Zack rubbed a hand across his mouth.

"Well..." Sunny nibbled her lower lip and crossed her arms, rubbing her elbows.

"Well..." Zack said, deeply regretting the turn things were taking, but knowing that it was the right thing to do. Without mutual respect, there was nothing. And he and Sunny Eden definitely did not share a mutual respect. "Yeah. Uh, well, good night, then, Doctor."

"Good night...Doctor." Taking a deep breath, Sunny turned and made her escape.

Zack watched until she stopped at a long motor home and unlocked the door. He was still watching several minutes later, after she'd gone inside.

"Well, well, well," Sunny murmured. "I guess you're not so highly principled after all, are you old girl?" She sighed and turned away from the mirror. Except for her top hat, she was dressed and ready to go to work. Ready at least in the physical sense. Mentally she was having a hard time summoning up her usual enthusiasm.

She was still kicking herself for being so easily swayed by her body's reaction to Zack Granger last night. He was rude, dense and archaic in his thinking—everything Sunny disliked in a man. He was also tall, dark, muscled and sexy—everything she did not dislike in a man.

But animal attraction did not a worthwhile romance make. Sunny knew that, had always known that. And yet it hadn't seemed to make any difference. That was the troubling factor in this equation. While Sunny believed in letting her heart rule her head from time to time, she did not believe in letting anything override her principles. So what, she wondered again, had come over her?

But she already knew the answer to that. It was Dan. She missed him so much. Missed the closeness of a man, the warmth . . . and the excitement. And the unexpected contact with Zachary Granger had caught her at a weak moment. It had been late, time to go home, and the nights were when the loneliness set in....

Sunny shook her head in an effort to shake off her thoughts. All of that business with Zachary Granger was over and done with, she decided, taking one last glance around the motor home. Today was a new day, and yesterday's mistakes were behind her. She was just glad she had put a stop to things before they really got started. Picking up her hat, purse and cash box, she stepped out into the early-morning sunlight and locked the mobile home's door behind her.

People were milling around their trailers, trying to wake up after another late night. Sunny exchanged greetings with a few of the carnival folks, but she didn't know any of them very well. She didn't travel with carnivals per se, she merely booked herself into whatever fairs and festivals appealed to her.

At times it was a lonely life, but it was an interesting one, too. She'd been traveling around the country for a year now, and while she didn't begin to imagine that she'd want to do this forever, she intended to enjoy the experience while it lasted. That was another thing Dan had taught her: to make the most of every day, every moment, every experience, because you never knew which one was going to be your last.

Her mouth curved in loving memory as she strolled along the slowly-awakening midway. Only a handful of fair customers were there; nearly all the activity came from the carnival barkers and ride operators. Everyone was setting up shop, hoping for a good, big-spending crowd. Sunny was hoping for the same thing as she unlocked the supply trailer and began taking out bottles and boxes.

"Miss Eden?" A small voice said.

Sunny turned in surprise, recognizing the teenage girl instantly. "Cheryl! My goodness, you're out here early this morning. Planning on a big day at the fair?"

The girl shook her mousy-brown head. "No, I just came to see you."

"Oh?" Sunny smiled, but there was an added alertness about her. "What can I do for you?"

The girl, about thirty pounds overweight, wriggled her hand into the front pocket of her too-snug Levi's. "I—I brought some more money. I wanted to buy a few more of your things...." She pulled out a wad of bills and showed them to Sunny, then clasped them tightly in her fist.

Sunny pressed her lips together, studying the girl. Cheryl had spent more than twenty dollars already, and now she was back, wanting to part with more of her money. Sunny recalled a certain male voice that had accused her of swindling the unwary—but that was not true. Whenever Sunny felt that a customer was buying more than he or she could afford or buying her merchandise for the wrong reasons, she did her best to put a stop to it. Looking at Cheryl, Sunny felt that the girl fit into both categories. She was spending too much and, possibly, trying to buy a friend in Sunny.

"I see," Sunny said, and sat down in her folding chair. "Well, what can I help you with?"

The girl shrugged self-consciously. "Well, I'm not sure. I just..." She looked at the ground, then back up at Sunny. "I just wanted to get some of the stuff that you use. You know, to make me look better."

The statement was so pitiful, Sunny felt a stab of sympathy. But she was careful not to let her feelings show. What Cheryl needed was respect, not pity.

"All right," Sunny said, seemingly all business. "Let's see...what do I use most?"

She cast a quick, appraising glance at the girl and tried to decide which products would give the best and quickest results. Teenagers were so easily discouraged. They wanted miracles, and they wanted them yesterday. But Sunny could sympathize. She remembered her own adolescence as being one of the most continually intense periods of her life. When you are fifteen, everything is a big, big deal.

"Okay," Sunny said, reaching for a large plastic bottle. "I use this shampoo every day. If I don't, my hair is so fine and limp, it just hangs in strings." She rolled her eyes, and noted with satisfaction that Cheryl was beginning to grin. There was always something cheering in knowing that other people had the same problems you did. "And this—" she set another bottle in front of her "—this is a natural astringent. It tightens up the pores and keeps my skin good and clean. And this—'' She leaned forward and lowered her voice conspiratorially. ''This is my secret weapon. I take some of these before I go to bed to keep the pounds from piling on. I swear, Cheryl, everything I eat anymore goes to my thighs...''

Cheryl chuckled and gingerly picked up a bottle on the counter. ''These help you lose weight?''

''They do me,'' Sunny said casually. ''Among other things. Of course, you have to eat right, too. And exercise. And drink plenty of water and get plenty of sleep. You know, there really is something to the old saying about beauty sleep. That's when the body renews itself—skin, nails, hair, muscle—the works. All of these supplements are just helpers, Cheryl. The real work is still up to us. The truth is that if everyone would just eat right and take care of themselves, we wouldn't need supplements at all.''

Cheryl was staring rather hungrily at the bottle of capsules. ''Okay, I'll take some of these. What else do I need?''

Sunny tipped her head to the side. ''Well, I don't know. What seems to be bothering you? What areas of your life do you need help with?''

The girl shrugged. ''I don't know. I just feel...'' She paused, dropping her gaze once again.

''Sick?'' Sunny suggested, already knowing the answer. ''Do you feel ill, Cheryl? Physically?''

"No." She shook her head. "I guess I just feel...ugly." She swallowed and couldn't seem to bring herself to look at Sunny after such a confession.

Sunny stifled the urge to hug her. A hug at this point would have them both in tears and would solve absolutely nothing. She folded her hands in front of her on the table. "You know, that's funny, Cheryl, because you look beautiful to me."

Cheryl snorted in self-derision. She had obviously been conned by well-meaning adults before and wasn't falling for it this time. After all, she could see in the mirror. Except she couldn't, Sunny thought. Like too many people, the girl could not see her own potential. She was just another diamond in the rough, and Sunny's fingers were itching to do some quick polishing.

"Really, Cheryl," Sunny said earnestly. "I mean it. Come here and sit down." She pulled a stool over and patted the seat. When Cheryl hesitated, Sunny insisted. "Come on over here, my friend. I'm going to show you what I see when I look at you."

As Cheryl made her way slowly behind the table, Sunny dug into her trailer for the box of supplies she kept handy for just such occasions.

Zachary Granger was in a foul mood. He hadn't slept worth a damn, and his head ached and his eyes felt scratchy. He lifted his coffee cup to his lips and poured more caffeine into his dragging body while he cursed Sunny Eden under his breath. Now the blasted woman was ruining his nights as well as his days.

He'd gone to bed thinking about her, and every time he'd managed to get to sleep, she had come to him in a nightmare. Of course, the dreams hadn't been nightmares while he was having them. It was only after he woke up that he realized how scary what he was dreaming really was. How could he honestly be attracted to someone like her?

It didn't make sense. He was an intelligent man, an educated man, and he didn't make a habit of acting on an animal level. But something about Sunny Eden seemed to bring out the beast in him all the way around.

He ran a hand through his hair and stared into his coffee cup. The solution to his problems with Miss Eden was obvious. Seeing her was dangerous—dangerous and foolish. If he kept locking horns with that woman, his self-respect would be in tatters. The only thing to do was keep his distance until the carnival left town. And pray, Zack thought, that the blasted female didn't talk his poor, gullible mother into joining the carnival right along with her.

"Voilà!" Sunny said, and held up a large hand mirror in front of Cheryl.

The girl stared at her reflection in wonder, her short, nail-bitten fingers touching her cheek to make sure it was really her.

"You see?" Sunny said, pleased with her handiwork. "You *are* beautiful, Cheryl. All you had to do was find it out."

The girl's smile was radiant. "I really look...okay, don't I?"

"Okay?" Sunny put her hands on her hips. "I beg your pardon, young lady. I don't see anything that's just 'okay' about you."

And that, Sunny thought, was the gospel truth. After she'd done Cheryl's makeup, she'd had another brainstorm. She'd closed up shop on the midway and whisked the girl back to the camper. There, she'd washed, cut and blow-dried Cheryl's hair into a feathery halo that did wonders for her rounded face. Even with the extra weight, Cheryl Evans looked absolutely radiant.

Her smile was lovely as she turned to Sunny. "Thank you...for everything."

"You're very welcome. I had as much fun as you did." Regretfully, she looked at her watch. "I hate to say this, Cheryl, but I'm afraid I'd better be getting back to work."

"I'm sorry. I didn't mean to keep you away from—"

"Honey, if I hadn't wanted to do it, I wouldn't have." Sunny brushed her hands on the seat of her pin-striped pants. "Why don't you walk me back to the Garden of Eden?"

Cheryl nodded eagerly and fell into step beside her. Sunny smiled with satisfaction, noting the new confidence in the girl's stride, the proud lift of her young chin and the Cheshire-cat smile on her pink-glossed lips. If Sunny didn't do a nickel's worth of business today, she'd have still had an excellent day's work.

When they got back to the booth, Cheryl waited while Sunny set up her display of goods, then the girl began picking out bottles and jars. "I want to get everything you used on me today."

"All right," Sunny murmured, and quickly selected what Cheryl would need to maintain her new look. When she came to the selection of natural diet aids, she glanced at Cheryl. "Do you really want to lose weight?"

Cheryl's head bobbed urgently. "Definitely. And I really feel like I can do it this time."

"Okay." Sunny nodded. "But remember, you have to diet and exercise to stay healthy and to look good. What do you like to do for exercise?"

Cheryl shrugged. "I'm not very good at sports. I guess I could do calisthenics..."

Which, Sunny thought, would probably only last a day or two. Unless a person could find something he really liked, maintaining a routine—especially alone—was pretty tough. Sunny raised her eyebrows as another brilliant idea came to her.

"Cheryl, how do you feel about running for exercise?"

"I don't know. I've never tried it." Her blue eyes ran enviously over Sunny's trim figure. "Is that what you do?"

Sunny nodded. "Mmm-hmm. Four or five times a week. Listen, I was just wondering if you'd like to come out here and run with me in the mornings until I leave town. By then, you'd be in the habit of doing it, and it will be easier to keep it up after I go—"

"That'd be great!" Cheryl said. "I'll be here in the morning. What time? And what should I wear? Will—"

"Just a second, Cheryl." Sunny held up a hand. "First things first. I want you to bring me two notes in the morning."

"Notes?" Cheryl frowned.

"Yes. One from your parents, giving you permission. And one from your doctor, telling me that running would be a good exercise program for you."

"I'm healthy," Cheryl protested. "And my parents don't care if—"

"Sorry," Sunny said, and meant it. Cheryl was a minor, and, as opposed to Martha Granger's case, Sunny *did* feel responsible. "Those are the rules, kiddo. Take them or leave them."

"I'll get the notes," Cheryl said. "I'll go home right now and start working on it."

"Good." Sunny gathered up the products Cheryl had wanted and put them in a plastic bag. "Here's your bag of tricks.'' She handed them to Cheryl. "Use all of them in very good health."

Cheryl dug in her jeans pocket for her money.

"Forget it," Sunny said. "This one's on me."

Cheryl gaped. "All of this? And the haircut and the makeover and—''

Sunny nodded and smiled. "On the house. Now go tell all your friends and neighbors how great my stuff is, and don't tell them you got yours free. I only do that for my very special friends—and my jogging partners. I'll see you tomorrow at my place around seven. Wear sweats or shorts or something comfortable and bring the notes. And, Cheryl? No forgeries, please.''

Cheryl laughed. "No forgeries, I promise. Both Mom and Dr. Granger will be glad to write me notes. Bye! I'll see you at seven."

And she was off.

Sunny stared after her, then closed her eyes.

Mom and Dr. Granger? she thought, groaning aloud. *Why is all this happening to me?*

Crystal Springs was too small a town for her even to open her mouth without creating more problems for herself. She could just imagine Dr. Zachary Granger's reaction when he heard that another one of his patients had been "conned" and "swindled" by Dr. Sunny Eden. And she had a feeling she knew Cheryl a little too well to think that the girl might not mention her name and what she'd been up to all morning.

There was a sudden tension between Sunny's shoulder blades. She flexed her muscles and tried very hard not to think about the probability of another run-in with Zachary Granger.

That, of course, was impossible.

Chapter Four

Okay, Brenda, who's next?"

The middle-aged nurse glanced at her clipboard. "Cheryl Evans. Room 3."

Zack frowned. "Cheryl? What's she in for?"

Brenda Higgins shrugged. "Doesn't say. Sherry squeezed her in between appointments, though. She said it was an emergency."

"Let's get to it then," Zack said briskly, and headed for room 3.

Cheryl was standing by the window, her back to him. "Cheryl," Zack said. "What seems to be the problem?"

She turned, and Zack felt his mouth drop open.

"Hi, Dr. Granger," the girl said brightly.

"Hello...." Zack was stunned. The Evans family had been patients of his father's for a couple of generations, and when Doc had died, they, along with most of his father's patients, had flowed into Zack's practice. He had been seeing Cheryl for the past few years, but looking at her now, he had the distinct impression that he'd never really seen her before at all. Gone was the shy, dumpy, insecure girl who would barely even look you in the eye. In her place was a lovely young woman.

Looking at her, Zack felt a mixture of emotions—surprise, obviously; happiness that Cheryl was finally coming into her own; and he also felt a grim disappointment in himself, because he never would have dreamed that this girl had such potential. Not just the potential to be physically attractive, but the potential to blossom into someone with such charming self-confidence and such an aura of personal contentment.

If he'd thought about her at all, he supposed he'd assumed she would always be the way she had been since he'd known her—awkward and sort of invisible. Yet, as her physician, he should have been more concerned with the whole patient—not just body, but mind and soul as well. He found himself wishing that he had had a part in Cheryl Evans's transformation and wondered what had brought all this about. A boy? A girlfriend? Cheryl herself? Zack didn't know, but whatever or whoever the cause, applause was definitely in order.

"Cheryl, you look terrific." And it wasn't really the makeup or the hair. It was in the spirit that was finally on the rise.

"Thanks, Dr. Granger." Cheryl beamed. "I feel terrific."

Zack sobered, suddenly remembering the reason for her visit. "You do? Then what brought you here? Brenda said you made an emergency appointment."

Cheryl blushed and lowered her gaze. "I hope you weren't too busy to see me." She looked up, appeal in her blue eyes. "It isn't really a medical emergency, but it is an emergency to me just the same."

Zack's gaze narrowed. Surely she wasn't pregnant or something? "Cheryl, I'm never too busy to see my patients. Suppose you tell me what this is all about."

Cheryl sighed happily, eyes sparkling. "I need for you to write me a note, Dr. Granger."

"A note?"

Her head bobbed, feathery hair dancing over her shoulders. "I need written permission to run. You know, a note saying that I'm healthy, etcetera."

"Run? You mean for a track team or something?"

"No." She chuckled. "To run—jog—for exercise. You see, I met this terrific woman at the fair, and she sort of... made me over today, and then..." She paused, her fingers twirling the ends of her hair while Zack's gaze narrowed further.

I met this terrific woman at the fair... Of course. It was the master of change and transformation, the voodoo queen at it again. First his mother, now Cheryl Evans. God only knew how many others she had gotten her hands on since she'd rolled into Crystal Springs—

Zack gave himself a mental shake and forced himself to concentrate on what the new and improved Cheryl was saying.

"...and then, she told me about these vitamins and things that help you lose weight, and then she asked me to run with her in the mornings until she leaves town. But she made me promise to bring a note from both you and my mother, or she won't let me run with her." Cheryl paused, out of breath. She took a deep breath and then blew it out. "Isn't that terrific, Dr. Granger?"

"Terrific," he murmured. "Did this woman know who your doctor was?" He couldn't imagine Sunny Eden being so worried about permission. After all that business with his mother, she had struck him as being thoroughly irresponsible, a person who acted first and thought later about the possible consequences. If, of course, she even thought about them at all.

"No." Cheryl frowned. "She didn't ask me about you or anything. Why?"

"Just wondered." Zack waved the question aside. "Let me have a quick look at your chart, then I'll give you your note."

To whom it may concern:

I see no medical reason for Cheryl Evans to refrain from running or jogging as a form of physical exercise.

Zachary Granger, M.D.

P.S. I do not endorse and have warned patient against unproven diet aids and supplements. Any pursuit of this matter is against my recommendation and therefore outside the realm of my responsibility as said patient's physician.

copy/file

Sunny read the note, then crumpled it into her fist. The little P.S. he'd added made her sound like some sort of dangerous quack diet doctor or something. She was half surprised that a note like that hadn't scared Cheryl off completely. But then, Sunny noted with a small smile, Cheryl was somewhat smitten with her newfound mentor.

The girl had arrived at ten minutes to seven, wearing a new gray warm-up suit and new white running shoes. At the moment she was following Sunny's instructions to the letter, doing knee bends and stretches to warm up for the main event.

Propping her leg up on the picnic table, Sunny started warming up, too, bending forward to touch her nose to her knee. Her hair was tied back with a red ribbon, and she wore a pair of well-used red sweatpants and a white sweatshirt with red trim. Her leather running shoes were almost worn through in a few places, but they were broken-in just the way she liked them, comfortable and cozy from lots of mileage.

"Okay," Sunny said, ten minutes later. "All set?"

Cheryl's head bobbed quickly. Sunny had the feeling the girl would have agreed to anything she suggested—not an entirely good thing, but something that would wear off after Cheryl's initial excitement toned down a little.

"Let's go, then, kiddo. We need to put some miles on those shoes."

"And take some pounds off these hips," Cheryl added with a laugh, and fell into step beside Sunny.

At noon, Zack left the office and walked down the hall to the kitchen for lunch. He supposed his mother had concocted yet another bizarre repast for his enjoyment. After just one afternoon spent with Sunny Eden, his mother's lifelong pattern of cooking and eating had been totally demolished.

Instead of pork chops, they had tofu and sprouts. Instead of bacon and eggs for breakfast, the Granger family now had millet and wheatberry muffins and papaya juice. Instead of coffee, his mother served herb tea. Zack's stomach rumbled hungrily. If this trend continued, he was going to starve to death. Of course, he thought with wry humor, he would at least die a very healthy man.

His mother was bustling around the kitchen when he entered. She glanced up and smiled merrily. "Hello, my fine, handsome young son. How was your morning?"

"Fine," Zack said, more than a little subdued. He did have to admit that after that first day with Sunny, when his mother had popped her cork, she had been more cheerful and contented than he had seen her in years. Grudgingly, he supposed that if nothing more came of the alliance with Sunny Eden than dabbling with health foods and taking a few vitamins now and then, it wasn't really all that bad. After all, it was worth something just to see his mother so happy.

And then there was Cheryl Evans. He also had to admit that Sunny had managed to do wonders for the girl's self-esteem and enthusiasm for life. And Sunny had taken time out from her work to spend with both his mother and Cheryl and who knew how many other dissatisfied souls. So maybe she really wasn't as much a self-serving con artist as he'd initially thought. Maybe she was just a decent, if slightly misguided, human being who was truly trying to help people in this world....

His thoughts were interrupted as his mother set a plate before him. He was unable to identify most of what he was supposed to eat.

"Today," his mother said, taking her seat across from him, "we're having zucchini fettucine as our main course."

Zack swallowed, feeling his appetite say goodbye. "Sounds great," he lied, for the sake of peace. "What's this?" He gestured to the glass of wicked-looking dark orange liquid she had set near his plate.

"Fresh carrot juice," his mother replied. "And I expect you to drink it. It's good for lots of things, and it's filled with important vitamins."

Zack groaned inwardly, biting his tongue so he wouldn't argue with his mother. These days there was simply no reasoning with the woman. He picked up his fork and gingerly poked at his fettucine while he made a mental note to let his mother know that he definitely had an engagement for dinner. He had a hot date with some real food—a thick steak, a huge baked potato and a crisp green salad. And right now, Dr. Zachary Granger couldn't think of anything that could possibly entice him to break that date.

It was five-thirty, and the action on the midway was a little slow. The day crowd had gone home for dinner, and the evening crowd hadn't shown up yet. Zack stood off to the side and a ways back from the Garden of Eden, hands shoved into the pockets of his tan slacks as he observed Sunny Eden and asked himself just one more time what he was doing there.

He supposed it had something to do with Cheryl Evans.... And, yes, he forced himself to admit, it also had something to do with his mother. There was just no denying that Sunny had helped them both to attain a new, more positive outlook on life. And Zack honestly believed in giving credit where credit was due.

Yet, he still had a problem with some of the wares she was peddling. Plenty of herbs and supplements could be dangerous in improper dosages and combinations. So he was also here to attempt to discuss that with her and convince her of the necessity of making her customers aware of potential hazards and also warn her of the dangers of making false claims. There were no quick miracle cures, and making the wrong claims to the wrong person could be psychologically risky.

So, Zack thought, nodding his head in satisfaction, *that's what I'm here for. To commend her on part of her work and inform and warn her on another part. Yes, that's it. Makes perfect sense to me.*

Yet he didn't feel as convinced as he wanted to, because he couldn't forget the fact that he'd driven to the fair almost unconsciously. And it had taken the past twenty minutes or so to figure out just exactly what his grand purpose had been in coming.

Before he could think about it any longer, he put one foot in front of the other and started walking slowly over to the Garden of Eden and the woman who inhabited it—Eve, the temptress, the instrument of man's downfall....

Sunny glanced at her watch and began packing up her goods so she could break for dinner. Sometimes she brought her supper in a brown bag, but in Crystal Springs, the five-to-seven-o'clock crowds hadn't really warranted sticking too closely to her post. She would take an hour or two off to wander around the fairground, then settle back in for a long evening's work.

She was locking the trailer when a man's voice drawled lazily from behind her, making her stiffen.

"Well, Dr. Eden, I guess this was mighty good timing on my part, wasn't it?"

Drawing a deep breath, Sunny took a second or two to compose her thoughts before she faced Zachary Granger. She really was not in the mood to argue with him tonight about Cheryl. If the blasted fool couldn't see that what she'd done for Cheryl was a good thing, then he was a . . . well, he was a blasted fool!

Lifting her chin, she turned around, and felt the breath catch in her throat as memories of a couple of nights ago danced through her system. He was a handsome cuss, no doubt about that. Dressed in tan slacks and a cream summer-weight sweater, he was standing on the other side of her now-empty display table.

"Hello, Dr. Granger," she said coolly. "Actually, I'm afraid your timing wasn't good at all if you came here to talk to me. I was just closing up."

"For the night?" A dark eyebrow lifted in surprise. Completely unbidden came the thought that she might have a date. Zack felt a new tension run through him.

"No," Sunny said, shrugging out of her vest. Beneath it she wore a white, long-sleeved blouse. For diversion, she concentrated on rolling up the sleeves. "Just for a break. But I really don't have time to argue with you about Cheryl Evans. I don't—"

"Well, that's good," Zack interrupted smoothly. "Because I don't have time to argue with you about her, either. That's not why I came here."

Sunny blinked. "It's not?"

Zack shook his head.

When he didn't volunteer the reason for his visit, Sunny prompted him. "Well, then? Why *are* you here?"

Zack opened his mouth to tell her, but nothing came out. After all the heated words he had exchanged with this woman, complimentary conversation suddenly seemed incredibly awkward.

"I, uh, well, I just stopped by to, uh..." He took a quick breath, then plunged on ahead. "I just wanted to say that I think what you did for Cheryl was...okay." There, it was out. Zack grinned in relief that the ice was finally broken.

But Sunny didn't look as pleased as he'd expected. She raised an eyebrow. "Okay? Gee whiz, Dr. Granger, you really know how to flatter a girl. I don't remember when I've ever received such high praise, and especially from such an impressive authority as yourself."

"Look," Zack said, exasperated, "I'm just trying to be nice here—"

"Try harder."

He put his hands on his hips and released a long breath. He had made an effort at decency, and she had slapped him down. He ought to just turn and walk away without another word. But the way she had responded to his compliment made him sound like some sort of pompous ass, and Zack wasn't about to leave while she felt as though she had the upper hand.

"Okay, Miss—Dr. Eden," he said evenly. "Because I'm a decent sort of human being and because I do believe in giving credit where credit is due, I will 'try harder.'"

He bent slightly at the waist and put his palms flat on the display table. The action brought him a little closer to her and put his eyes on the same level as hers, which, Zack discovered too late, was a big mistake.

Remembered sensations sizzled along his nerves. His recall was graphically complete as images of the night he'd caught her by the arm and gazed into her green eyes flashed through his mind. He felt hot and cold and nearly desperate to have her in his arms. Good Lord, she really had to be the most beautiful woman he'd ever met.

"Well?" Sunny prompted, crossing her arms. "I thought you were going to make another stab at being nice?" Her skin felt feverish, and the ice she was trying to inject into her voice and manner was doing absolutely zip to cool her down.

She couldn't remember the last time a man had had such a devastating effect on her—wait, yes she could remember. When she'd first met Dan, she had felt this same way. Sunny trembled inwardly at the realization.

Long ago she had resigned herself to the knowledge that she would never experience that wonderful, overpowering, nearly scary attraction again. But here it was, by golly, as strong and surprising and exciting as ever... and caused by a man with whom there was absolutely, positively no hope of a future. Good grief, Sunny thought sadly. With him there was not even any hope of having a present, much less a future.

So she forced herself to get a good solid grip on her emotions. She straightened her posture and took a small step backward, away from the magnetic force that kept trying to draw her in.

Zack was still gazing at her silently, and Sunny felt positive that he was experiencing the same chemical reaction to her that she had to him, hence his long silence. If things had been right between them, words would not have been necessary. But under the circumstances, Sunny thought that words, the right words, were absolutely essential to breaking the spell.

"Look, Doctor, I can see that this 'nice' business has really got you stumped." She grabbed her purse and slung it over her shoulder. "So I'll tell you what

I'm going to do. I'm going to take my break now. You stay here and keep trying to think of what you're going to say, and then say it to me when I get back. You'll have to think fast, though, because I've only got about—" she glanced at her watch "—an hour and a half. If you don't think you can come up with anything by then, you could always sleep on it and come back tomorrow."

One corner of Zack's mouth curved upward. "You know something, lady?" he drawled, eyes narrowed. "You've really got a smart mouth on you."

"And a mind to go with it," Sunny retorted. *Which is why, she thought, I'm going to get out of here while the getting is still good. You're dangerous to me, Zachary Granger, and I'm not going to let you make me forget it.* "If you'll excuse me, Doctor, I really have to go...."

Zack stood up straight and dusted off his hands. Outwardly he was calm, but inside he was grasping for a way to spend more time with her. It wasn't something he could rationalize, but when it came to Sunny Eden, his mind kept bowing out and letting his instincts and emotions take control. He couldn't seem to help himself.

"Wait," he said, then plunged on before he could change his mind. "I just wanted to say that what you did for Cheryl was...impressive. I really mean that. I just couldn't get over the change in her."

Sunny paused, meeting his gaze warily. "Well, thank you, Doctor. I appreciate your saying so."

Zack shoved his hands into his pockets. He kicked at a rock on the dusty ground. "I also wanted to say that my mother seems very happy right now. A little strange maybe, but happy. She, uh, seems about ten years younger. Like maybe she's found the, uh, fountain of youth . . . or something."

Touched by the confession, Sunny looked down and closed her eyes briefly, feeling a small smile come to her lips. She met Zachary Granger's gaze warmly. "Or something," she murmured. "I'm glad."

"Yeah." Zack chuckled, feeling some of his tension finally being released. He ran a hand through his hair. "I'm glad, too. I guess. I have to admit, though, this whole thing still makes me a little nervous."

"That's understandable," Sunny said graciously. "It's a whole new way of thinking for you. I'm impressed, Dr. Granger, that you've begun to see the other side. Most doctors I've run into are positively thickheaded on this subject, a fact I've never been able to understand. I mean, it only makes sense to me that a health-care professional would be interested in all kinds of health care." She shook her head. "Unfortunately, though, that's usually not true."

Before Zack could reply, his stomach grumbled loudly, reminding him that he had a date with a steak. He grinned crookedly as Sunny's raised eyebrows told him she had heard his belly's rumbling complaint.

He patted his flat stomach. "Sorry for the interruption. I had sort of a light lunch."

Sunny tipped her head to the side while her mind raced to determine whether or not she was about to do something she would regret. Considering the past few days, it did seem rather likely, but then again, the past few minutes had been encouraging. And truth to tell, she really did not want this conversation with Zack Granger to end. It seemed they were on the verge of a bona fide breakthrough, and Sunny couldn't help wanting to see it firmly cemented.

"Actually, I was just going to dinner myself," she admitted. "You're welcome to join me, if you like."

For a split second she thought he was going to refuse. Then his mouth widened into a white smile that positively dazzled.

"Dr. Eden," Zack said, "I thought you'd never ask."

Chapter Five

There was very little food on the carnival midway that Sunny considered suitable for human consumption. While she didn't consider herself to be a picky eater, she could see no valid reason for feeding an incredible machine like the human body substances that would do nothing to help it and plenty to harm it. By the time she finished regaling Zack with horror stories about the hot dogs and French fries and cotton candy he kept eyeing, he had pretty much lost his appetite for carnival fare as well.

Exasperated and starving, he stopped near a cart of gleaming candy apples and glared at her. "Okay, okay, okay, you win, Doctor. We won't eat any of this junk. But I'm telling you, I've got to eat something soon.

You just pick something that you won't lecture me on and point me to it. Now.''

Sunny laughed. "All right, I get the message. Let's see." She looked around, biting her lip. "To tell you the truth, I usually eat at home. If you'd like, I could whip something up."

Zaçk nearly pounced on the suggestion. Then he remembered where his mother had been getting all her new recipes and nearly groaned aloud.

Yet the fact remained that he really wanted to be with Sunny just a little bit longer. And the prospect of the privacy of her motor home was just a little too enticing to turn down. Smothering a sigh for his long-suffering stomach, he settled for the best meal he was going to be able to get. After all, there was more to life than food.

"That sounds great." He hoped his smile wasn't as weak as it felt. "Really great."

Sunny grinned. "Follow me, Doc. That body of yours is in for a treat."

Zack followed. "Great," he mumbled under his breath. "Really, really great."

"Hey," Zack said, raising an eyebrow. "This really is great."

Sunny laughed and picked up her brimming glass of iced mint tea. "I told you that you were in for a treat. Why so surprised?"

Zack shrugged and slid the char-grilled shrimp, mushrooms, pineapple, green pepper and cherry tomatoes off the skewer and onto his plate. This was the best shish kebab he could ever remember having eaten in his life. Maybe it was just because he was so incredibly hungry. And then again, maybe it was because his dinner companion was proving to be excellent company. Sunny Eden was a lot more than just beautiful. She was bright and quick and funny and...

Zack cleared his throat and forced his train of thought to take a different track. He knew that he was fast becoming well and truly smitten with the woman as it was. Dwelling on the fact at this point just somehow didn't seem wise. In truth, he kept hearing an inner voice cautioning him to do as little thinking as possible, just to sit back, relax and enjoy the moment for what it was. Because this pleasure, he knew, was a temporary pleasure. All the more reason to savor it....

He took another bite of the succulent shrimp and grinned at Sunny. "This is really, really good. Why is it, Dr. Eden, that you never gave my mother *this* recipe?"

Sunny blinked, then laughed as she began to get the picture. "Has your mother been trying out some of the things I told her about?"

Zack rolled his eyes. "I'll say. Every time I sit down at the table, it's something a little more bizarre—unique, I mean."

Laughing, Sunny clapped her hands, then rested her chin on her tented fingers. She was having an absolutely marvelous time. They were outside, sitting at the picnic table in the shade of a big old leafy tree while the lowering sun painted the rest of the campsite with a golden glow... a golden glow that Sunny felt had gone right inside her and was radiating back out.

Her eyes felt as though they were sparkling like a crystal Colorado lake, and the laughter that Zachary Granger kept evoking from her felt like warm honey in her throat, smooth and rich and natural and wonderful.

And who'd have thought? Sunny mused dreamily. Who'd have ever thought that conversation with this particular man would ever be anything but tense and frustrating? Who'd have thought that she would ever find such a pure and natural pleasure in his company without something physical taking place...?

She dropped her gaze as her warm glow suddenly got warmer. Good heavens, he was really something. Her lips felt dry, and the tip of her tongue slipped out to moisten them. Zack stopped talking about his mother's cooking, trailing off in midsentence. She looked up to find his gaze on her mouth, dark eyes lazy and glittering.

"Please," Sunny said nervously. "Go on. I was listening. You were talking about the fettucine and carrot juice your mother gave you for lunch today...."

Unconsciously, she licked her lips again. And immediately regretted it. His gaze was like his kiss would be—hot, thorough and exciting. Sunny fumbled the napkin from her lap and dabbed at her mouth.

"So..." she said, forcing a bright smile. "How was it?"

"How was what?" His voice was lazy, with a husky edge.

"The fettucine. You know, the lunch you were complaining about a minute ago." She took a long swallow of her iced tea, welcoming the coolness and wishing she could take a bath in it.

"Awful. But the carrot juice was the worst yet."

"It is a little strong," Sunny said, finding it hard to believe that this inane conversation was taking place. There were suddenly so many powerful undercurrents running between them, it was almost impossible to think about anything else. So she rattled on, at a loss as to what else to do.

"I remember the first time I tried carrot juice, I nearly gagged. But it grows on you, it really does."

"Yeah," Zack murmured. "Like a fungus."

Her laugh sounded brittle. "More or less, I guess." She drained her glass. "I think I could do with a refill, how about you?" She stood up, needing a minute or two away from him to catch her breath and get her reactions under control.

"I'm okay," Zack said, lifting his glass to show it was still half full.

"Okay. Be right back."

She scurried away, escaping into the cool privacy of the motor home. She caught a glimpse of her reflection in the mirror on the closet door and stopped, staring. She had the look of a lovestruck teenager on her twenty-eight-year-old face. Her cheeks were flushed, and her eyes were positively glowing with an inner excitement.

Absently, she touched her fingers lightly to her cheek. Was this really her? Was this the widowed woman who had believed that she had already known, loved and lost the only man who could cause her to look this way, to feel this way...?

"Hey, Doc?" There was a quick rap on the door, then Zack was climbing into the motor home. He had to duck a few inches to keep from skinning the top of his head on the aluminum door frame.

Self-conscious, Sunny spun to face him. "Something wrong?"

Zack rattled the ice cubes in his glass. "Decided to take you up on that refill after all."

"Oh. Okay. Sure." Glad for something to do, Sunny went to the refrigerator and fished out the plastic pitcher of mint tea.

A second later Zack was behind her. Sunny stiffened, sucking in her breath and holding it while she waited to see what he intended to do. He wasn't touching her... yet. But she swore she could feel the entire length of his body against her. She closed her eyes, not daring to move.

She was confused. She didn't know how she was going to handle what was about to happen. She didn't know what she wanted to happen. There was a deep, age-old desire to simply relax against him and go with whatever seemed natural and right. But there was also the age-old instinct that insured the survival of any species—the instinct for self-preservation.

Right from the start she had known that Zachary Granger was dangerous to her. And now, especially now, she knew why. Something about him had the power to involve her and make her care. And that gave him the power to hurt her.

Zack Granger could never be a casual encounter. There was nothing casual about the way she felt around him. Whether she was angry or amused or intrigued or aroused, the emotion was not casual. It was intense, full force, full-bodied, something she hadn't really experienced since Dan. Something she hadn't really expected to experience again.

And she didn't honestly know if she was ready to experience it again. Until she knew, she had to stop things before they got started.

"Zack, I—"

"Watch your head," he said.

"What?" Sunny frowned.

Above her, Zack was opening the freezer door. "Watch your head." When she still didn't duck, he placed a large palm on the top of her head and gently pushed her down so he could get the freezer door open.

"What are you doing?" Sunny's mind was running in low gear. Part of her was still occupied with trying to reject Zack's advance without making him feel that she wasn't interested in him. Because she definitely was. She just needed some time to think about things, to decide how she really felt about getting deeply involved with someone at this stage in her life.

"I'm getting the ice," Zack said dryly. "And you, Doctor, are supposed to be getting the tea. Or did you forget what we came in here for?"

No, Sunny thought. *I didn't forget. I came in here to cool off a little, and you... you came in here to warm things up.*

Or had he? Sunny tightened her grip on the pitcher and slipped sideways away from Zack. Maybe she had read him wrong. Maybe he hadn't used the tea as an excuse to be alone with her in the camper. Maybe.... But, no, Sunny thought, as she caught a glimpse of his face out the corner of her eye. He was feeling the effects of their closeness in the small motor home, too. Yet he had pulled back just when she had. Which meant he had either anticipated her withdrawal or he had reservations of his own.

"Of course, I didn't forget what we came in for," Sunny said, recovering slightly now that she was not so close to him. "I may be ninety-three, but I'm certainly not senile—yet."

Zack shot her a dry glance, memories of their first meeting obviously darting through his mind. "I'd like to see you at ninety-three. You'd probably be just as feisty as you are now."

"More so, I imagine." Sunny grinned, feeling more at ease. She didn't know Zack's reasons for letting the mood of a few moments ago disintegrate, but she appreciated the reprieve just the same. "As I would guess you've figured out by now, I don't believe that age automatically dictates much change. Youth is a state of mind."

"Youth is a state of body. And you cannot will a seventy-year-old body to do what it could do at twenty. Now come on, Doctor, admit it. There is more difference between the two than just the way we imagine ourselves. Even you can't argue with that. Some things you just have to accept."

"Obviously." She watched Zack drop ice cubes into the glasses. "But some things you don't have to accept. Like a dull, boring life-style that someone else, or society in general, wants to impose on you."

Zack pressed his lips together, thinking of his mother. He exhaled heavily. "Agreed." He refilled the ice trays and replaced them in the freezer.

"Or a program of health maintenance that may be accepted by the general medical community, but may or may not be the right program for you."

Zack watched her fill the glasses with the green herb tea. When he didn't answer, Sunny tipped her head back to look up at him.

"Right?" she prompted.

Zack shook his head. "I don't know. I suppose that I do agree with you in theory. But I'll just be real honest with you, Sunny..."

It was the first time she could remember him calling her by her first name, and the husky sound of it curled her toes.

"Yes?"

A small frown made creases in his brow. "The truth is that the prospect of your ideas as reality scares me half to death."

Sunny frowned in surprise. "But why? I don't understand that kind of attitude."

Zack sighed. "I know you don't. That's why I'm going to take as much time as is necessary to make you understand." He took the tea pitcher from her and put it back in the fridge. Then he picked up his glass and used his free hand to take her by the elbow.

"Come on," he said. "Let's get this thing resolved once and for all."

"Okay," Sunny said, resting her elbows on the picnic table. "Shoot. Explain to me, if you can, why doctors refuse to recognize so much of the progress that's being made."

Zack shook his head. "I can't speak for everybody else. I suppose everyone has his own reasons."

"And yours are?"

"Mine are . . ."

He paused, collecting his thoughts. It seemed imperative all of a sudden that he make her understand, that they come to some kind of a mutual understanding. Looking at her, he knew he did not want them to remain on opposite sides of the fence any longer.

Their time together was short. Sunny would be leaving when the fair ended—but Zack didn't want to think about that. A lot could change between now and then, but he wasn't going to allow himself to think about that, either. Yet. There was still a lot standing between them, and if there was no hope of resolving their differences, there was certainly no hope of anything else.

Resting his forearms on the table, he leaned toward Sunny. "First of all, I do acknowledge the validity of herbal remedies and vitamin therapy, etcetera. I hadn't thought about it in years, but my mother reminded me that even my dad used to prescribe that kind of thing for his patients when it was appropriate. So, unlike most medical doctors, I have been exposed to holistic medicine."

"Then why did you have such a fit about your mother buying my stuff?" Sunny frowned.

Zack shrugged. "I don't know. Primarily because she's my mother, I suppose. She'd spent two hundred dollars, at a carnival, on a bunch of stuff I'd never even heard of. She'd taken a stranger's advice about what to use to cure her ills and make her young again. In short, Doc, I felt she'd been conned."

Sunny nodded, understanding why he would have felt the way he did. He was a good son, loving and protective of his mother's health and finances.

Absently, Sunny traced a crack in the wooden table. "And now?" She glanced up, knowing his response was more important to her than she wanted to admit. "Do you still think she'd been conned?"

There was a brief hesitation. Then Zack shook his head. "Not exactly, no. As I told you before, my mother has definitely benefitted from her dealings with you."

Sunny sensed a hesitancy in the admission. "However..." she prompted.

"However," Zack said. "I'm bothered by this whole alternative-therapy business for one main reason." He frowned and met her gaze, hoping he could get through to her. "Look, Sunny, the thing is, I'm worried that once people get started on home remedies, they'll rely on them exclusively—which is great, unless you're talking about someone who really needs medical treatment. I've seen people refuse surgery and die of a cancer that might possibly have been operable. I've seen people decide that their children didn't need treatment, and I've seen children die."

Sunny looked down. "And I've seen someone follow the doctors' orders to the letter, without even looking into alternative treatments, and die three months earlier than the six months that was predicted."

Zack watched her, seeing the pain of loss that was etched into her beautiful features. She had lost someone very dear to her. Mother? Father? Someone close. He hurt for her.

"I'm sorry," he said softly. "I know that happens. Sometimes the best you can do just isn't good enough."

She met his gaze. "And sometimes maybe a different alternative would give better results." She pushed her hair back. "That's all I'm saying, Zack. That people should be informed of all the options before they make their decision about treatment. And it should be their decision."

"Maybe you're right," he admitted. "God knows, the medical profession does not have all the answers. Personally, I'm not opposed to looking in new directions." His mouth quirked wryly. "Now, that is. I'm ashamed to admit that I'd settled into the comfortable groove of what I know, what I've been taught. Instead, I should have been looking for answers to questions that nobody's solved yet. Comfort leads to nothing but mediocrity." He laughed, silently and wryly, shaking his head. "I used to know that—back in my younger days. I guess I should thank you for bringing my original purpose in life back to my attention.''

Sunny's smile was warm and tender. ''Thank you, Doctor. For having a noble purpose and being willing to take it up again. We need more doctors who have more questions than answers. We need more people who have more questions than answers.''

His hand skated over the few inches of picnic table to pull her fingers into the warmth of his. He couldn't remember having felt this good in years.

Good Lord, he didn't want her to leave.

''You know,'' Zack said thoughtfully, as he and Sunny strolled along the neon-lit midway, hand in hand, fingers threaded cozily together, ''the answer is to combine the two—your way and my way. Then patients can get the best of both.''

Sunny turned to glance up at him. She felt so good she could have hugged every person she came in contact with. Zachary Granger was better than any tonic in the world. Strolling along with him, she felt alive and vital and . . . loved, something she hadn't felt in a long, long while.

''Combine the two how?'' she asked, anxious to hear his ideas.

''I don't know.'' He shrugged. ''But there has to be a way. Maybe every medical office should have a resident witch doctor to—''

''Resident what?'' Sunny demanded.

He laughed, a warm, smooth sound that rippled pleasantly over her nerves. "A resident...person like yourself," he amended, dark eyes glittering with amusement and affection. "An expert in your field. Then, when a patient comes in, you and I could have a conference and fight it out until we agree on the best form of treatment for that particular case..."

He went on, expounding on the same theme, but Sunny wasn't listening anymore.

You and I could have a conference...

What had started out as a general, undeveloped, impersonal notion had very quickly bloomed into a very specific, very personal—*what?* A proposition? An invitation to join his practice? To work side by side with him every day?

But, no, Sunny thought quickly. That was ridiculous. He had just been speaking hypothetically. Zack Granger was not the type to jump into an arrangement like that on the spur of the moment. He would have to think long and hard before inviting someone into his medical practice. The care of his patients wasn't something he took lightly. He was merely playing with ideas....

"So," he said. "What do you think? Would it work or not?"

Sunny thought about it in general terms, because, of course, that was what Zack meant. Yet she couldn't keep her imagination from toying with the image of her and Zack, side by side, working together to save the world....

"Sure, I think so," she said. "I mean, I don't see why not. If both parties were determined to be open-minded, I think it would be a wonderful thing. And you could set up a program for patient education—"

"Which you'd be good at," Zack inserted. "I've seen the way you work those crowds."

"I don't 'work' them," she said, not liking or agreeing with the implication of manipulation. "I entertain them. I have fun with them. And, maybe most importantly, Dr. Granger, I like them."

His smile was warm. "I know that now. You really, genuinely do like people."

"Don't you?"

"Sure, when I think about it. But I guess somewhere along the way I just sort of forgot how to enjoy the general population." He shook his head, then paused near the ticket booth for the double Ferris wheel. He turned to face her and looked down into her eyes. "You know what I like about you, Dr. Eden?"

"I'd be afraid to guess." But she felt breathless to know.

"The fact that you have a way of making me think about things that I haven't thought about in years."

Sunny smiled. "I'm glad. That's what it's all about, Doctor. Using our minds instead of going through the motions like automatons."

He nodded and sighed. "Yeah. Now, do you want to know what I don't like about you?"

Sunny frowned. "Not particularly, but I'm sure you'll fill me in. What don't you like about me? And I'm warning you, Doctor, I haven't got all night."

He smiled. "The fact that you have a way of making me think about things that I haven't thought about in years."

She laughed. "Uncomfortable at times, isn't it?"

"And embarrassing. But worth it. Like I said earlier, comfort breeds nothing but mediocrity." He grabbed her other hand so that he was holding both of hers in a warm, firm grasp. "Now, what do you say we give the shoptalk a rest and ride this big wheel?"

Sunny looked up at the bright yellow-and-green lights of the double Ferris wheel. From where she stood, the top wheel looked as though it could nearly reach the clouds. But then again, looking at Zack, Sunny felt like she could nearly reach the clouds without ever leaving the ground.

"Love to," she murmured, and Zack walked over to buy the tickets.

"Sunny! Sunny!" a young, cheerful voice called over the noise of the midway.

Sunny frowned slightly until she recognized Cheryl Evans threading her way toward the Ferris wheel. Cheryl Evans and a tall, rather handsome young man.

"Cheryl," she said with a very pleased and self-satisfied smile. "How're you doing?" *As if I can't tell,* Sunny thought smugly. The girl was positively glowing. Her eyes had the look of... Well, Sunny admitted, her eyes had the same look that her own had had when she'd caught a glimpse of her reflection in the motor home's mirror.

"Terrific." Cheryl beamed. "I'd like you to meet Jake, Jake Scott. We, uh, go to the same school."

"Nice to meet you, Jake," Sunny said, and wished she could have seen the boy's face when he'd first gotten a glimpse of the new Cheryl. As Cheryl finished the introductions and they made the usual small talk, Sunny noticed that Jake's gaze kept sliding appreciatively to Cheryl. He seemed quite taken with his date.

Cheryl sparkled, carrying the conversation and taking her rightful place in the spotlight. She was in the middle of a sentence when Zack returned with the tickets to the ride.

"—and then, we—Dr. Granger!" Cheryl said, surprised. "Hi. I wouldn't have expected to see you here." Her gaze went from him to Sunny. It took a second for the conclusion to dawn on her. Her eyes widened. "Are you two... together?"

Zack grinned and slipped an arm around Sunny's shoulders. "So far we are," he said dryly. "Right, Doc?"

Sunny had to swallow past a sudden tightness in her throat. She could smell the musky scent of his aftershave and wanted to melt against him. Forever. But, like the doctor had said, they were together . . . so far.

Who knew how long the good feelings were going to last? But one thing she did know was that she didn't want to spoil the wonder of the moment with worries about the future. After all, the moment was all you ever really had.

"That's right, Doctor," she murmured. "So far."

Chapter Six

The lights of the fairground and some of the town surrounding were spread out below them like a modern-day glittering fairyland. There was calliope music and rock-and-roll and adolescent shrieks. There was a cool, fresh, Rocky mountain breeze, and there was the musky-spicy scent of Zack, his arm around her shoulders while the top wheel of the double Ferris wheel tumbled lazily forward and the bottom wheel paused to change passengers.

"This is great," Zack said, slouching comfortably in the padded seat. "I don't think I can even remember the last time I went on a carnival ride."

Sunny gave him an arch look. "If I were you, I

don't think I'd admit that, Doctor. You're showing your mental age."

One corner of his mouth lifted. "Are you trying to tell me something? Like maybe I'm stuffy and boring?"

"Boring? You?" She shook her head. "I don't think you could ever be boring, Doctor."

He lifted his chin, puffing up a little. "Whether you meant it that way or not, I'm going to take that as a compliment."

"As was intended, of course." Sunny nodded innocently, although there was a bright sparkle in her green eyes. "You'll notice, however, that I didn't get into the 'stuffy' issue."

"I noticed," Zack said, and sighed. "Oh, well. I guess you can't have everything." Tapping his fingers lightly along the metal back of the seat, he gazed around at the view. "Beautiful, isn't it?"

Sunny followed his glance. "Mmm-hmm. It really is—"

She paused as the seat started rocking, lightly at first, and then more violently. The little metal bucket was swinging wildly as they crested the top of the wheel. Her stomach somersaulted.

"Zack! Stop it!" She grabbed the front of the bucket, knuckles white.

Zack laughed, white teeth flashing. He felt about fourteen. It was summer vacation, Friday night, and

he had a cute little blond cheerleader at his side...
Ahhh, the memories.

Ahhh, the pleasure of being an adult and yet still
having the old thrills to go along with the present ones.

His arm tightened around Sunny, but he kept on
rocking the bucket. And laughing. And feeling fabulous. She was laughing, too, and yelling at him at the
same time. Her eyes were sparkling, and she clutched
at him instead of the cold metal, her hands slipping
around his waist, her head pressing against his shoulder.

Zack put his other arm around her and held her
tight. He stopped rocking and closed his eyes, savoring the moment. This night, Sunny Eden had given
him what had to be one of the world's greatest gifts.
She had given him access to the child in himself. And
as he breathed in the clean scent of her hair, he silently swore that he'd never lose that part of himself
again.

It was the part that took sheer joy in the simple
things, making every day a little bit magical. It was the
part that made you want to accomplish grand
things... and made you believe you could. It was the
part that let you fall in love, purely, simply, totally—
instantly—and made you believe that it could last a
lifetime. And finally, it was the part that allowed you
to do things impulsively, without thought for the future or the consequences or the possible complications or anything else.

It was that part that let him slide a hand around the side of Sunny's face and lift her chin for his kiss.

It happened so naturally, the way their lips came together. Sunny didn't take time to think—only feel. His mouth was warm and mobile, testing at first, then increasing in pressure to become exploratory. Tongues mingled, and Sunny's senses exploded. There was nothing but Zack, the feel of him, so warm and lean and male, and the smell of him, musky, clean and exciting, and the taste of him as she clung to the kiss, to the moment, wanting both to last forever.

It was with shared reluctance that they finally drew apart.

A little dazzled, Sunny drew in a long, shaky breath and let it out slowly. "I do apologize, Dr. Granger."

Zack nodded in satisfaction. "Apology accepted, Dr. Eden."

Their wheel was now at the bottom and was slowing down. As their seat reached the ground, two young men with long hair and deep tans caught the bucket and let them out.

One of the men gave Zack a tired look. "Next trip, lose the rocking, buddy. House rules."

Zack laughed and nodded as he led Sunny away.

Her knees were weak. In fact, her whole body felt weak and tingly. She clung to Zack's arm for support as they left the big, wonderful double wheel behind.

Kissed at the top of the Ferris wheel. It was a romantic classic.

When, Sunny wondered, was the last time it had happened to her? High school, she guessed. But she knew for certain that she had never been so thoroughly kissed back then. In fact, there were very few times in her adult life that she had been kissed like that—hotly, passionately, yet very, very sweetly. A combination guaranteed to rock her senses.

"Hey, you two! Wait up!" It was Cheryl and friend, hurrying up behind them. They had been right behind them on the ride, too, Sunny remembered belatedly. She wondered if they had seen the kiss, then quickly decided she couldn't care less. Her relationship, or whatever she had with Zack, was not a secret. And besides, the fair was for lovers.

Cheryl's blue eyes were twinkling knowingly. "Enjoy the ride?"

Sunny glanced at Zack, wondering whether he would feel that the incident would detract from his professional image. He was grinning nonchalantly.

"Loved it," he said easily, and slid his arm around Sunny's shoulders. "How about you two?"

"Great," Cheryl said.

"Yeah." Jake grinned. Apparently he was the strong, silent type. Following Zack's lead, Jake slipped his arm around Cheryl.

"We were just wondering," Cheryl said, "if you two would want to do the rest of the rides together? You know, like a double date."

Sunny raised her eyebrows in surprise. "I would think the last thing you two would want would be to have a couple of old folks like us tagging along."

Cheryl shook her head, her freshly washed and curled hair bouncing around her shoulders. "Yeah, but you guys are different from most people your age. Besides," she said quickly, "you're not really old anyway. Right, Jake? We think it would be fun, don't we?"

"Yeah." Jake bobbed his blond head earnestly. "Really."

Sunny slid an amused look at Zack. The Ferris wheel had been a spur of the moment thing. She didn't really think that "doing the rest of the rides" would be something he'd be interested in.

"Well, thanks, Cheryl, Jake," Sunny said. "It sounds great, but we—"

"We'd love to," Zack interrupted smoothly. "Unless, of course—" he challenged Sunny with a look "—you're not up to all the excitement?"

"Me?" She put a hand to her breastbone. "I'm always ready for a little excitement. In fact, I don't think there is enough excitement in this world to satisfy me, Dr. Granger."

Zack's smile was lazy, his eyes heavily lidded to shield the sudden promise in them. "Maybe we'll just

see about that one of these days," he murmured for
her ears alone—ears that began to burn as his mean-
ing sunk in. "But for now, I guess we'll just have to
settle for some carnival rides."

They did them all—the Zipper, the House of Hor-
rors, the House of Glass and the Salt and Pepper
Shakers. They rode the carousel with the little children and the old folks, and they literally threw their
money away on the nickel, dime and quarter pitches
and came away with more ashtrays than four non-
smokers could ever use.

Zack and Jake threw baseballs and tossed basket-
balls and hurled footballs and won cheap stuffed ani-
mals and ropes of gaudy plastic beads. Sunny and
Cheryl strode along, chins high with pride as they
toted their plush bounty and twirled their new jewels.
And they did indeed feel like genuine jewels, Sunny
thought as Zack draped yet another strand of plastic
around her neck and Jake did the same for Cheryl.
Wondrous baubles from two adoring suitors....

"There," Zack said. "If this won't keep you around
a few more days, I don't know what will."

Cheryl perked up at the statement. "Are you going
to stay for a while, Sunny?" she asked eagerly. "After the fair leaves, I mean?"

Sunny opened her mouth to speak, but nothing
came out. She certainly hadn't dared to think that far
ahead. In fact, with Zack Granger, she'd barely dared

to think two minutes ahead. Their relationship had a way of changing to extremes instant by instant.

"I—I hadn't thought about it," she finally admitted. But Zack wanted her to stay for a few more days. What did that mean? What did she want it to mean? And, of course, the big question, the real toughie: what did she want him to mean to her?

"Where were you planning on going next anyway?" Cheryl wanted to know.

Sunny was too aware of Zack's alert silence. "Uh, Pueblo, I think. Yes, Pueblo."

"That's only about sixty miles from here," Jake inserted. During the course of the evening, he had loosened up considerably.

"Yeah," Sunny said brightly. "An hour's drive. That's not too far."

Too far for what? she wondered. To commute? To see Zack? What for? After Pueblo she was off to the Midwest. Definitely out of commuting distance. No, if she left at the end of the week, she would be gone. Just plain gone. If not for good, at least for a good long time. So if she went, she'd better be sure—

Sunny blinked, suddenly becoming aware of her thoughts. *If she went?* What did that mean? It meant, she realized, that she really was thinking about staying on for a while. A part of her longed to stay on for a while. The main draw, of course, was Zack. And he would have been enough. But there was even more. There was the beautiful little town and the mountains. And then there were her new friends—Cheryl and Jake and Martha and...Zack. There was Zack. And he was enough.

He was studying the dusty ground, his handsome face unreadable. But when he looked up, there was a challenge in his eyes. "What's the matter, Doctor?" he murmured. "Chicken?"

Sunny's eyes widened. "I—"

"Chicken?" Cheryl frowned. "Of what?"

"Of nothing," Sunny said, shooting Zack a warning look. She couldn't believe he was saying this in front of their teenage audience.

"Of a lot of things," Zack said. "I'm beginning to think that the good Dr. Eden doesn't practice what she preaches."

"I do, too," Sunny said, although she wasn't precisely sure of what he was talking about.

"You do not," Zack said easily.

Cheryl and Jake glanced from one to the other, shifting uncomfortably.

"Uh, Cheryl," Jake said. "You want to go get a hot dog or something?"

Cheryl, noticeably curious, was a little reluctant. "Yeah," she said. "Sure. I'll go with you, but I'm not having anything. Diet, you know. Be back in a minute, you two."

"Okay." Sunny watched them wander off, then she turned to Zack. "All right, Doctor. What was all that about?"

Zack shrugged. "Just stating facts, Doctor. Just stating facts. You make a habit of telling people to go for the gusto, go after what they want, live a little, take a chance, put a little spice in their lives."

"So?" But Sunny didn't like where this whole conversation was leading.

"So," Zack said patiently, "you're not practicing what you preach. You and I both know that we've got the beginnings of something that could turn out to be very interesting going on between us. Yet you don't seem to be very willing to stick around awhile and give it some time to see how things work out. As a matter of fact, I've been getting the distinct impression that the whole idea of something working out scares you to death."

"That's not true," Sunny said automatically, but her head was spinning at the direct approach that Zack was using. He was interested, and he wasn't wasting any time on the preliminaries. But then again, Sunny realized, they didn't have much time. And all he was proposing was that she give it a little time. That was hardly a request for a major commitment. If she lived in the area, this whole conversation would never have come up. Things would have just taken their natural course and either blossomed or fizzled out.

"Really?" Zack's low voice interrupted her thoughts. "If it isn't true, then prove it. Stick around, Doc. At least stay for the fireworks."

Sunny licked her lips. She felt awkward and nearly panicky. She had to fight the urge to wring her hands in agitation. Zack was right: she was scared. Really scared that something powerful and lasting would develop. Or that it wouldn't.

"I—I don't know," she admitted. "I'll have to think about it."

Think about it she did, for the next two days. It was particularly easy to think about it—because Zack never showed up. As she worked, Sunny kept scanning the crowd, looking for a dark head. When she took her breaks, she was keyed up, half expecting him to pop out of nowhere as he had done in the past, but he didn't. At night she lay in bed tossing and turning and listening for his footsteps outside the motor home. But they never came.

So what was he doing? she wondered. Giving her time and space to think clearly? Spending some time alone to sort out his own feelings? Staying away because he'd changed his mind? Or was he doing this to drive her crazy? To prove to her that she was as nearly addicted to him as he'd suggested that he was to her?

"Oh, just shut up!" Sunny growled to her whirling mind.

She pulled her pillow over her head and willed herself to go back to sleep. It was five in the morning, and she had been up half the night, thinking, wondering...panicking. If she stayed, there would be no walking away. This much she knew. She was already half in love with the man, and every day brought her just that much closer.

Was that what she wanted?

She and Dan had been college sweethearts. He had been her first and only serious relationship. When he died, a part of her had simply shut down. It was the part in her that longed for closeness, for a meaningful partnership. It certainly hadn't been a deliberate decision; it had merely happened. And it had been comfortable. A little lonely, maybe, and not particularly fulfilling or exciting, but fairly comfortable just the same.

And comfort, Zack had said, *only breeds mediocrity.*

Sunny squinched her eyes shut, trying to block out her thoughts. Her work, the travel, her life, had all been pretty interesting and uncomplicated until she'd rolled into Crystal Springs. Now, whether she stayed or left, it would never be quite the same. Zack had stirred something to life that she'd thought dead and buried, and she had the feeling that it wasn't going to settle back down for a long, long time.

She flopped onto her back and lay there, going over her dilemma over and over again. She only stirred when there was a knock at the camper door.

Her heart jumped, but when she glanced at the clock and saw that it was quarter to seven, she knew who it was. Cheryl. Bright and early as usual. They had another jogging date. And she wasn't even dressed.

"Just a minute," she called, and scrambled out of bed, pushing her sleep-tangled hair out of her eyes as she went to the door. She unlocked it and pushed it open, then swung around to hunt for her sweats.

"Come on in, Cheryl," she tossed over her shoulder. "I'm sorry, but I'm running a little late this morning. If you want to have a seat, I'll—"

She stopped talking. Something was wrong. She could feel it. Or maybe it was just her imagination....

She bit her lip and turned slowly around.

And there, in her entryway, was Zack.

"Morning," he said.

Sunny pushed her hair back again and held it in place. "Uh..." She had to swallow, and there was a dry click in her throat. Had she thought he was handsome? He was not handsome.

He was devastating.

Dressed in worn gray sweats, he was obviously just out of the shower. He smelled clean and vital and wonderful, even from a few feet away.

"Good morning," she managed, and crossed her arms over her stomach, self-conscious in her icy-pink silk nightshirt. It covered her well enough, hanging nearly to midthigh, but she still felt naked. Behind her was her unmade bed, and before her was Dr. Zachary Granger, the man who had kissed her at the top of the

Ferris wheel. The man who had challenged her to stay and be with him for a while....

Was she crazy? What on earth was she having a problem about? He really was quite fabulous.

"I wasn't expecting it to be you," she said.

"I know. You thought it was Cheryl." He shrugged and gave her a crooked half smile. "If you'd known it was me, you probably wouldn't have let me in."

It was her turn to shrug. "I probably would have. I just would have taken a minute to make myself a little more . . . presentable."

He laughed softly, nearly silently. "Doc, if you have something that can make you any more presentable than you are right now, you ought to bottle it and market it. You'd make a fortune."

The male appreciation in his voice and his eyes fired her skin. "Excuse me a minute, will you? I'm going to put on a robe."

She turned, hoping he hadn't seen the flush in her cheeks. She slipped on her white chenille robe and felt much more composed when she faced him again.

He shook his head slowly. "Hate to disillusion you, Doc, but you do not look more presentable."

Sunny cleared her throat and lifted her chin. Thank heaven, her wits were returning. "And I hate to disillusion you, Doc, but that's just too darned bad." She shook her hair back. "Now, what can I do for you? What brings you out to the fair at this hour of the morning?"

And what brings you here after two long days of absence? Am I supposed to be thrilled that you're finally gracing me with your presence? Am I supposed to be angry that you wasted two days, two precious days that could have made a big difference in my ultimate decision? Am I supposed to be afraid that you're going to tell me that the other night was all a mistake, that you got caught up in the moment and spoke before you thought? What am I supposed to be right now?

Zack's eyes narrowed slightly, trying to read her. "Why, Doc, I would think it would be obvious what I'm doing here." He gestured to his clothes. "I came to see if I could find myself a couple of jogging partners."

Just like that? Sunny thought. That's it? No explanation for the absence? No reference to his challenge of the other night?

"Jogging partners?" she echoed, stunned. "I didn't know you were a runner."

Zack folded his arms across his broad, flat chest and leaned back on his heels. "I do believe in keeping in shape, Dr. Eden. I've been running for years."

Which was true, Zack thought, to a degree. He could see no point in mentioning that lately he had fallen out of that habit from his youth as well as too many others.

He just couldn't stop thinking about how good this woman was for him. He honestly felt like a kid again.

When he'd first seen her, she had been touting her products as the fountain of youth. Hell, *she* was the fountain of youth. At least for him. And all he wanted to do was drink from that fountain until he was sated. And he had the feeling that that could take a very long time.

"So," he said. "You mind if I join you?"

Sunny had to fight the urge to shake her head and clear her thoughts. Apparently, Zack wanted to back up to where their relationship should have been if he hadn't jumped the gun—the polite, rather innocuous, getting-to-know-you stage. But didn't he know that that would never work? Not now!

However, it seemed best to play along. "Sure. You can join us if you like. Cheryl should be here any minute." She stood looking at him for a second, trying to figure him out. "I really need to get dressed now, Doctor. So if you'll excuse me . . ."

Zack nodded. "Sure. I'll just step outside and wait for our little friend."

"Great," Sunny said, still staring.

"Great," Zack said, and stepped cheerfully out the door.

"So what do you think of Sunny, Dr. Granger?" Cheryl paused in her warm-up stretches to tip her head to the side and eye Zack knowingly.

Zack wasn't warming up. He was sitting at the picnic table, long legs stretched out in front of him, back resting against the tabletop. "Well, I don't know, Cheryl," he said. "What should I think of her?"

Cheryl grinned and windmilled down to touch her toes. "I guess if you're as smart a man as I always thought you were, you'd probably know that she's pretty terrific."

"Yeah?"

She put her hands on her hips and twisted from side to side, working on her obviously thinning waistline. "Yeah," she said. "In fact, if you're as smart a man as I always thought you were, you'd probably even be thinking about trying to keep her here by asking her to marry you or something."

"Or something," Zack murmured, then chuckled. "Cheryl, you do realize that I only just met her a few days ago."

Cheryl shrugged. "How long does it take?"

"How long does what take?"

"Falling in love," she explained with forced patience. "The way I've always heard it, it can happen in an instant."

Pretty much, Zack thought wryly. That's pretty much the way it happens. But what he said was what he had always thought in his pre-Sunny days.

"That only happens in books and movies, Cheryl. Real life isn't quite that way. I mean, you have to get to know a person. Spend some time together. Find out whether or not you have anything in common—"

He broke off, knowing he wasn't kidding himself or Cheryl. When they'd first met, he and Sunny had had absolutely nothing in common. Yet, looking back, Zack had the feeling that he had started on that famous 'fall' the first time he'd seen her.

Cheryl gave him a dry look, wise beyond her years as young people and children often are. The wisdom, of course, came from brutal honesty, the kind most people quickly learn to outgrow.

"Mmm-hmm." Cheryl murmured. "Sure, Dr. Granger. Whatever you say."

Zack frowned and studied Cheryl more closely. The girl he'd known before this week would never have had the nerve to treat him as though he was babbling nonsense, even if he was.

"You know, Cheryl, I just can't get over the change in you. You seem like a whole different person."

She flashed him her sparkling new smile. "I am a whole different person. And I like me now, thanks to Sunny."

"I can tell," Zack said. "It's great that you're so happy. And, by the way, just in case nobody's told you yet this morning—you look beautiful."

Caught off guard, Cheryl paused jerkily in her toe touches. Her cheeks flushed crimson. "Actually, Jake told me that when I met him for breakfast—well, he had breakfast and I had ice water—but, thanks, Dr. Granger. I don't think a girl could ever hear that too many times in one morning.'' Or one lifetime, Cheryl thought dreamily.

You're beautiful. It was something that people had never said to her before, something she'd never felt about herself before. And now, since Sunny, people were telling her that all the time.

And they meant it, too. Cheryl could tell. All her hard work was paying off, too. Every day when she got on the scales, her weight was down. Whenever she had tried diets before, nothing had ever done the trick.

But now that there was more pleasure in her life than food could ever provide, dieting was a breeze. Sometimes she didn't think she cared if she ever ate again. After all, compliments from men like Dr. Granger provided a lot more sustenance than candy bars and Cokes. Not to mention how much better they were for her complexion....

Her thoughts were broken as the camper door opened and Sunny stepped out, looking terrific, as usual, in her red-and-white sweats. Her normally glowing skin looked even more glowing today, and Cheryl knew the reason why. Her blue eyes slid from Sunny to Dr. Granger and then back to Sunny.

Cheryl wasn't the only one who had come to love Sunny Eden. And Cheryl wasn't the only one who was dying to think of a way to make her stay in Crystal Springs. And not just for a while, either. Forever. There were at least two people in the little town who needed Dr. Sunny Eden very, very much.

Chapter Seven

Sunny wasn't at all sure that she wanted to be needed by anybody for anything. For years now, she had made a point, albeit unconsciously, of being independent. And making sure that no one else became too dependent on her.

Zack was right, of course. She was chicken. She was yellow from the top of her shiny blond head to the bottom of her pink-polished toes. Once upon a time she had walked blithely into love and commitment and emotional dependence and all the rest and expected it to last a lifetime. Which, she guessed, it had. It just hadn't lasted her lifetime. And the shock of it all had nearly done her in.

However, she was a survivor, and she had found a way to survive on her own, with plenty of pleasant acquaintances and no potentially painful strings. Now Crystal Springs was threatening that. People were becoming attached to her, and she to them.

As they ran—herself, Cheryl and Zack, circling the outer boundaries of the fairground—Sunny kept sneaking glances at her two companions. And, oh, how pleasant it was to have companions. She doubted she would ever run by herself again without feeling a little lonely.

Cheryl, as usual these days, was beaming, flashing Sunny smiles of what came dangerously close to adoration. She had come to really care for Sunny, and, blast it all, Sunny knew that she had come to really care for the girl. Cheryl was like the little sister she'd never had.... And Zack, well, Zack was Zack.

She watched him as he rounded a corner a little ahead of her. The sleeves of his sweatshirt were pushed up, revealing tanned, sinewy forearms that glistened with sweat. He was a beautiful male machine, all power and grace and precision, floating along with her in perfect harmony, matching her stride for stride.

He turned and caught her watching him. "This is great, isn't it?"

"Sure is," Sunny said, and meant it. Why couldn't she have more of this? she demanded silently, feeling suddenly angry at the injustice of it all.

Yet no one was stopping her but herself.

If someone came to her and told her that they had loved and lost and were scared to death of getting involved again, what would she tell them? She'd tell them, in no uncertain terms, to stop moping and go for it. In fact, she was constantly telling someone to "go" for something.

And she meant it and believed in it, really she did. But it was truly a tough thing to do. Which was why, of course, she got so excited and thrilled when she saw someone else accomplish what she herself had never been able to summon the nerve to do: put the past behind her and build a real, blood-and-guts-and-emotion-filled future for herself.

Maybe it was time.... Maybe she *would* stick around for the fireworks.

They were nearing the camping area, and Zack began to veer toward it.

Sunny frowned. "Hey! It's this way, remember?"

Zack glanced over his shoulder. "What's that way?"

"Our route. But we can go a different way if you want to."

Zack's brows drew together. His legs were aching and cramping up, and he was struggling so hard not to pant that he thought his lungs were going to burst. How had he gotten so out of shape so fast?

"What do you mean?" he asked, still running and puffing a little. "How far do you run?"

"Usually four or five laps. But you can quit if you need to."

Four or five laps? Around the whole fairground? Zack smothered a groan. So far, they had made one lap. One, single lap. He might make two, but four or five would probably land him in the emergency room.

But it wasn't Zack who wound up in the E.R. It was Cheryl.

It started in the middle of their second lap. Cheryl stumbled, cried out and fell. Zack and Sunny were instantly at her side, helping her up. But Cheryl was not conscious.

Sunny felt the girl's limp body and saw the whites of eyes that had rolled back in Cheryl's head, and she felt her knees buckle and a sickening, vomitus weakness roll through her.

"Oh, God, Zack! What's wrong with her?" On her knees, she clutched Cheryl's hand, willing her to be all right and fighting the fear that the girl was going to die or something.

"I don't know," Zack said briskly. "Here, move back. Let me lay her down and take a look. You get to a phone and call an ambulance."

"An ambulance?" Sunny croaked. Zack was supposed to be telling her it was all right. Good Lord, the man was a doctor. If he thought an ambulance was necessary, it must be really bad....

"Go, Sunny!" Zack said tersely, while his skilled fingers examined Cheryl. "Now! Run!"

His firmness gave her limbs strength. She ran, arms and legs pumping wildly, mind going blank of any clear thought except one. *Get to a phone. Save Cheryl.*

Thankfully, it was a small town and the hospital wasn't very far away. By the time Sunny had made the call and run back to Cheryl and Zack, she could hear the approaching siren. The shrill sound chilled her as it always did, but this time, there was a degree of comfort in knowing that whatever and whoever was on board might be able to help Cheryl.

She plunged onto her knees, next to Zack, panting from the run and the fear. Cheryl's eyes were still closed. Her face was sheet pale.

"How is she? Did anything happen while I was gone? What's wrong with her?"

Zack spared her a glance. "I think she's going to be okay. She came around some while you were gone, but I told her to rest."

Sunny stared at the girl. "She's going to be all right?" she echoed, grasping at the assurance. "So we don't need the ambulance?" It seemed to her stunned mind that if they didn't need the ambulance, everything would be okay.

"It's just a precaution," Zack said, and put an arm around her trembling shoulders. "If we'd been farther away, I would have taken her in my car. But everything's so close here, I'd rather be safe than sorry."

Sunny bobbed her head jerkily. "Right. Safe. That's...that's good. To be safe."

Zack pulled her more tightly against him. "It's gonna be okay, Doc. Really."

"Really?"

"Really."

Sunny believed him.

She hated hospitals. In those long, terrible last days, she had spent too much time in a hospital, smelling the antiseptic, smelling the sickness and the worry and the grieving. Smelling the death.

She hadn't been near a hospital or a doctor's office since then, three years ago. But when she entered the emergency room, the last time she'd been in a hospital could have been yesterday. All the old misery hit her like a physical blow.

She grabbed for the back of a molded plastic chair while Zack went about the business of getting Cheryl admitted. The girl's mother was on her way. Zack had radioed the hospital to call Cheryl's parents. There was nothing Sunny could do but stay out of the way and let the professionals do their work.

Cheryl had come around in the ambulance. She was weak but conscious, thank God, and soon they would know what had happened. Sunny fought off present fears and past memories and forced her mind into a blissful blank. Carefully, she eased her way around to the front of the chair and sank into it. To wait. And watch. And wonder. And pray.

"Sunny?" A gentle hand was on her shoulder.

Startled out of her thoughts, Sunny looked up. Martha Granger smiled comfortingly into her face.

"Martha, hi. What are you doing here?"

The older woman sat down next to her. "Zack called me. He said you were pretty shaken up and that you might need a friend."

Sunny smiled, warmed by his thoughtfulness and Martha's quick trip to the hospital. Even though it seemed like hours since they'd brought Cheryl in, a glance at the clock told Sunny it had only been about ten minutes.

"Thank you for coming," Sunny said, grateful for the company. A hospital waiting room had to be the loneliest place in the whole world.

"I was just glad Zack thought to call me," Martha said. "Sometimes that boy does surprise me."

"Me, too, Martha," Sunny said. "Me, too."

She smiled softly, thinking of their long, wonderful evening at the fair. The good times seemed like a year ago, and she missed them, however brief they had been. If only they could go back, back before Cheryl had gotten hurt, and somehow change the course of history. But Sunny knew only too well that the past existed, no matter what, and could never be changed.

"Martha," Sunny said, searching the woman's eyes for the truth. "Did Zack say anything about Cheryl? Do they know what's going on yet?"

Martha shook her graying head. "No, not yet. They hadn't really had a chance to check her out. But he did say that he didn't think it's too serious. Of course, they'll probably have to run a few tests, that kind of thing, just to be sure."

Sunny nodded, feeling better. It had crossed her mind that Zack might have been sugarcoating his preliminary diagnosis just to comfort her. But she doubted he would do that with his mother. The woman had been a doctor's wife for years. She was used to dealing with the harsher realities. Sunny began to relax and once again felt grateful for the woman's presence.

"Thanks again for coming, Martha. Zack was right. I did need a friend." And the incredible thing was, she actually had a true friend in this little town she'd only rolled into a few days before. In fact, she had three honest-to-goodness friends, a luxury she hadn't allowed herself in a long time. A luxury that felt very, very good right now.

"Coffee?" Martha asked, getting up from her seat.

Sunny shook her head automatically. "No, thanks. I don't drink the stuff."

Martha rolled her eyes. "That's right. I don't, either, anymore." She chuckled. "Funny how old situations bring about old habits, isn't it?"

Sunny nodded, smiling a little.

"Okay, scratch the coffee," Martha said. "How about some juice or something? There's a machine just around the corner."

"That would be nice," Sunny decided. "I'm afraid I don't have any money. I didn't have time to go get my purse."

"I have plenty of change," Martha said. "And I'm going to see if I can't find out the latest on Cheryl's condition from one of the nurses. Wish me luck."

"Luck."

Martha walked off, all business and confidence in this place of sickness and smells.

But it was also a place of healing, Sunny told herself silently. Everyone who checked into a hospital did not die like Dan had. There was help here for many.

She let the thought settle in and forced herself to pay attention to her surroundings rather than try to block them out as she had done since her arrival. Everything was all business, running like a well-oiled machine.

The nurses and attendants were busy, but not harried, and the longer Sunny looked, the more the scene had a calming effect. Maybe it was time she changed her views on hospitals as well. Her last experience had been devastating, but this one was going to be good.

Cheryl was being well taken care of with Zack guiding the troops. She had the whole place and all its people and sophisticated equipment at her disposal. So, yes, Sunny thought, this could be a good place to be.

She forced her mind to continue on this positive track. There were other good things here, too. On one floor, babies were probably being born this day. New mothers were getting their first glimpses of the precious little cargo they had been carrying for the past nine months. New little lives were beginning, seeing this big, amazing world for the first time with wide-eyed wonder.

Sunny bit her lip, feeling a pang of envy steal through her. If she kept up the way she'd been going these last few years, she would never know the joy of bringing a new life into the world and of nurturing and loving it as mothers have done since time began. She, who preached about living life to its fullest, would miss out on one of life's most precious rewards. One of many precious rewards.

A picture of Zack came to mind as Martha made her way back and sat down. She handed Sunny a bottle of pineapple juice.

"Thanks," Sunny said. "Any news about Cheryl?"

Martha nodded. "She's doing great. Still a little weak, but we can go up and see her for a minute if you want to."

Sunny jumped up. "Of course, I want to! Let's go."

As they neared the elevators, Sunny glanced at Zack's mother. "Did they find out what's wrong with her?"

Martha's gaze skittered away. "Yes, but the nurse was vague about it. Zack said it's nothing to worry about at all, though. They're going to let Cheryl go home in the morning."

"Thank you, God," Sunny whispered, and followed Martha Granger into the elevator.

It was spooky walking into Cheryl's room. Sunny again felt a sickening sense of déjà vu when she saw the girl in bed with an IV poking into her arm. How many days and nights had she sat in a room so similar to this and watched Dan waste away right before her eyes?

But—Sunny blinked and shook her head to clear it—this was now. This was Cheryl. And Cheryl was going to be just fine. This was actually a joyous occasion.

She took a deep breath and walked to the girl's bedside. On the other side of the bed, a thin, pale woman looked up at her, tense, unsmiling. Cheryl's mother, Sunny thought, and felt very sorry for the woman and the scare she'd been through this day.

Cheryl smiled. "Sunny, hi. I'm sorry I messed up our laps. I guess we'll just have to do twice as many the next time, huh?"

Sunny laughed and felt dangerously close to tears. "You bet. I swear, some people will do anything to get out of exercising. Cheryl, how are you feeling?"

"I'm okay now. For a while there, I was a little scared. I didn't know what was going on. But I only fainted. Now I just have a little bit of a headache, and Dr. Granger says that's normal."

"Great," Sunny said. "I'll tell you, kiddo, you sure had me worried."

"Cheryl." The older woman stood up and met Sunny's look coolly. "I think you'd better rest now. The doctor said you could only have visitors for a minute or two."

"I didn't hear him say that," Cheryl frowned. "And besides, I'm fine, Mom, really. I want Sunny to stay. Oh," she said, looking quickly from Sunny to her mother. "I didn't introduce you two. Mom, this is Sunny Eden, from the fair, the one I keep telling you about—"

"I know who she is." There was a distinct chill in the woman's voice, and Sunny's eyes widened in confusion.

"It's nice to meet you, Mrs. Evans," Sunny said, trying to be especially cordial to the obviously tense woman. Probably she hadn't yet gotten over the shock of seeing her child in the hospital bed. "You have a wonderful daughter. She and I have become very good friends."

"Really," the woman said tightly, then suddenly her control crumpled. She glared at Sunny while a sheen of tears brightened her eyes. "I'd like you to leave now, Miss Eden, just leave my daughter alone. You've done enough damage here today."

"Mom!" Cheryl said, shocked. "What are you talking about?"

"Lie back, Cheryl." Without taking her eyes from Sunny, she patted her daughter's shoulder. "You're supposed to rest. It's time for your...visitors to leave."

"But, Mom!" Cheryl said again. "You can't just—"

"Cheryl." It was a sharp warning sound as her mother transferred her attention to her daughter. "I want this woman to go! Now! It's all her fault that this happened to you, that you're here, sick—"

Sunny sucked in a breath.

"That's not true!" Cheryl declared, sitting straight up. She glanced at Sunny in apology, then looked back at her mother. "That's not true at all."

"It is," Mrs. Evans said. She was shaking, evidently striving for control.

Sunny said quietly, "I don't understand, Mrs. Evans. Why do you think it was my fault that Cheryl got sick?"

The woman sniffed. "Cheryl didn't just get sick. She made herself sick by buying all your vitamin pills and following your advice about exercising."

Sunny felt a large knot form in her stomach. "I—I don't understand. Nothing that I suggested to Cheryl should have hurt her—"

"Oh, really?" the woman interrupted. "My daughter hasn't eaten one bite of food since the day you 'made her over.' She's been living on nothing but your stupid vitamin pills and exercising hours and hours a day. She said she was finally able to stick to a diet, thanks to you. Dr. Granger said the reason she collapsed was too little nutrition and too much exertion. You, Ms. Eden, are a health hazard. And I want you to know that I'm looking into the feasibility of filing charges or a lawsuit or something. I don't want you endangering someone else's child!"

As the woman spoke, tears filled Sunny's eyes.

"Mother!" Cheryl was pale with shock, anger, mortification. "Not one word of that is true! Sunny never told me not to eat. In fact, she told me what and how much I needed to eat to lose the weight and stay healthy. She even gave me recipes, and... Going on the fast was my decision—all mine. I never even mentioned it to Sunny or Dr. Granger because I figured they'd tell me to take it slower. I just didn't want to take it slower. It was all my idea—all my fault."

Mrs. Evans stood for a minute, studying her daughter. "Is that true? She never told you to go on this fast?"

"No!" Cheryl was emphatic. "And she was careful about the exercise, too," Cheryl continued, seeing her mother begin to calm. "Remember? Before she would even let me run with her, she made me go see Dr. Granger and get notes from him and you, too, giving me permission."

Mrs. Evans bit her lip. "That's true. I . . . had forgotten that." She took a long breath, then looked at Sunny. "I'm sorry, Ms. Eden. I didn't fully understand. And . . . it's been a difficult day."

Sunny nodded, her throat almost too tight to speak. "It's—it's okay. I understand." She smiled weakly at Cheryl. "I'll see you a little bit later. I think you should probably rest."

She left the room as quickly as she could, a baffled Martha Granger scurrying along behind her.

As they waited for the elevator, tears began to stream down Sunny's cheeks.

"Sunny, don't," Martha said, frowning in concern. "Don't let Marilyn Evans get to you like this. She was wrong about you, and she realized it. She was just upset."

"I know," Sunny said. "I know." But the woman's statements and accusations kept flying through her head.

Cheryl hadn't eaten in days, not one thing, a total fast. And while fasting could be very beneficial, there were right ways to do it, and there were wrong ways to do it. Cheryl had done it the wrong way.

So why hadn't she picked up on what Cheryl was doing? Why hadn't she asked more questions? She had known that the girl was overzealous and anxious for quick results. She had also noticed that Cheryl had become visibly thinner over the past several days—an awfully quick weight loss that should have served as a warning.

So why, she demanded of herself, hadn't she asked?

But she knew the answer. The fact of the matter was that she had been too involved in her own affairs to worry about Cheryl's. Since that evening with Zack, she had thought of little else.

And a teenage girl had collapsed because of her negligence.

Sunny closed her eyes and leaned back against the wall. She felt Martha's cool hand close around her own, but she was unable to derive much comfort from the gesture.

Martha's insistence that the woman had been out of line in blaming Sunny went unheeded. The fact remained that there had been signs, clues to Cheryl's actions, and if she had only been paying attention, she would have seen them.

Cheryl had trusted her, and Sunny had let her down. Mrs. Evans was right. She was dangerous.

And Zack had known that the first time he'd met her.

"Come on, Sunny," Martha urged, tugging at her elbow. "Let's go." The elevator opened. "Let's go find Zack."

Sunny froze. "No," she murmured. "I—I can't right now. I—I have to get to work. Yes, I have to get to work."

The truth was, she had to avoid Zack at any cost. There was no way she could face him after what her negligence had done to Cheryl. It could have been worse, so much worse. If Cheryl had passed out while riding a bike. Or taking a shower. Or darting across a busy street—

Sunny swallowed hard. No, she couldn't face Zack and see the look of disgust in his eyes. The disgust she felt for herself was sickening enough.

As the elevator doors closed behind Martha, Sunny darted for the stairs.

"She what?" Zack demanded, grabbing his mother by the shoulders. "Mom! How could you let her do that?"

"I couldn't stop her," Martha declared. "I thought she was following me into the elevator. Next thing I knew she was racing down the hall to the stairs. She was white as a ghost, too, Zack. I think Marilyn Evans really shook her up."

"No kidding," Zack said, running a hand through his hair. He knew how Sunny must be feeling. Good Lord, she was so caring about people. And then to be told that she was responsible for Cheryl's collapse—it must have nearly killed her. He glanced at his watch. "How long ago did you say that was?"

Martha shrugged. "Ten, maybe fifteen minutes ago, I guess. I don't know. I didn't look at the clock. I was running around here, trying to find you. I—"

"Okay," Zack interrupted. "Okay. Now, you said she said she was going back to the fairground? Back to work?"

Martha nodded. "That's what she said, but I think it was just an excuse."

"Okay," he said, rubbing his hand over his mouth. "I'll check her camper first. Keep your fingers crossed, Mom. That crazy blonde is going to be the mother of your grandchildren one of these days."

Martha gaped and watched her son's broad back as he strode quickly down the hall. She blinked and gaped some more. Then she smiled faintly and shook her head. Sometimes she was so darned proud of that boy, she wanted to cry. He was a smart one, her Zack. Darned smart. She only hoped Sunny Eden was as taken with him as she was.

Chapter Eight

His fist banged the aluminum door one more time.

"Sunny! Open up! I know you're in there."

He knocked some more. He had been banging on the door for the past five minutes. The truth was, he did not know if she was in there. Actually, the chances were that she wasn't, or she'd have said something by now.

But he didn't know where else to look. He'd checked her booth on the way in, and there was absolutely no sign of recent action. Besides, she hadn't been dressed for work. And Zack seriously doubted she was in the mood to work anyway.

So where was she?

He pounded again until his knuckles were sore. "Sunny!" he shouted, just in case. "Come on, I just want to talk to you!"

"Well, that may be," a male voice drawled. "But it looks to me like the lady don't want to talk to you."

A pair of men—the speaker about fiftyish and his friend in his early twenties—had appeared at one end of Sunny's motor home. They stood watching Zack through narrowed eyes, their bodies drawn in lines of challenge. The older man had his hands on his hips, fingertips in the front pockets of a pair of worn Levi's, while the younger man had his arms folded across a bare, deeply tanned and muscled chest.

Zack looked heavenward and sighed. Two knights in shining armor were all he needed right now.

"Look, fellas, you've got the wrong idea about this. I'm a doctor, and—"

"And that means you got a license to practice medicine," the older man said. "And that's *all* you got a license to do."

Zack's mouth tightened in exasperation. "You don't understand. Something happened over at the hospital, and Sunny—the lady—was upset. I just need to—"

"I think you just need to leave her alone. If she wanted to talk to you, I reckon she'd probably open the door. Don't you?"

"Not necessarily," Zack began, then stopped. This was totally fruitless. "Look, just forget it. She isn't home anyway." He walked past them, conscious of their steady gazes. A few steps away, he stopped and turned around. It was stupid, he knew. But he went ahead and took the chance. "I, uh, I don't suppose you've seen her in the last half hour or so?"

No response. Just stony looks and stonier silence.

Zack blew out a breath of disgust. Why couldn't the fools see that he was only trying to help her?

He headed back to his car and wondered where on earth the good Dr. Sunny Eden might have gone.

It was a good two minutes after the voices had stopped before Sunny could bring herself to come out of the bathroom. The plastic vent above the shower had been open, and she had heard everything that had transpired between Zack and her would-be protectors. She was rather touched by the gesture from her fellow travelers, but their action hadn't really solved her problems, it had only postponed them.

Still, that was all she had been trying to do when she'd hidden in the shower. The time would come when she'd have to face Zack eye to eye....

Or would it? Sunny bit her lip as a new idea came to her. It was a cowardly idea, she supposed. No, it was a cowardly idea, she *knew*.

But the more she thought about it, the more it seemed like the only way out. She'd die inside if she had to see the look that would be in Zack's eyes.

Lord, how she loved him.

She knew that now, accepted it for what it was and all that it could have been. But things had changed, and being willing to stay with him and give love a chance would no longer be enough. Not for Zack anyway. Not after what she had let happen to Cheryl.

He looked everywhere: in the parks, along the picturesque little streets of the town, in the shop windows, everywhere he could think of that a person could go if she was traveling on foot.

Of course, she could have gotten a ride somewhere. There were buses and a few cabs, but somehow Zack didn't think she would have caught a ride. She'd been upset, and he felt fairly certain that Sunny Eden would be the type to work off her emotions with physical exertion. Of course, in the shape she was in, Zack thought dryly, she could be halfway over the Rockies by now.

He swung the car around and made another loop around the park. Little kids were on the swings and slides and belly-crawling through the pipe tunnels while their mothers kept one eye on them and the other on paperback books or lapfuls of knitting.

Zack smiled wryly, thinking of Sunny. If she were one of those mothers, no doubt she'd be grubbing it up right alongside the little crumb-crunchers. He could just see her, blond hair falling in loose tangles as she wrestled on the ground, coming up laughing and grass-stained and—

His fingers tightened on the wheel. He had to find her. Comfort her about Cheryl and about Marilyn Evans's ridiculous accusations.

Then, he had to convince her to stay.

It was amazing how quickly one could pack up and pull out, Sunny thought as she eased the motor home and trailer off the on ramp and into the flow of traffic. It was the tourist season, and traffic on the interstate was fairly heavy as families made their way to or from whatever dandy vacation spot they had selected for this summer.

Cars drove past with luggage strapped on top and kids and souvenirs and oodles of junk packed into the back seats. Busy little arms and legs and mouths seemed to move a hundred miles a minute while moms kept turning around to smile or scold or hand back a sandwich to reaching fingers.

It all looked very hectic and trying.

It all looked very wonderful.

Sunny's mouth tightened, and her foot got a little heavier on the gas. She wanted out of here and out of here fast. Crystal Springs and all that went with it was behind her now. And the more miles she could put between that place and herself, the better off she was going to be.

Period.

End of discussion.

Too bad, though, that it was only the beginning of more than a few tears. She blinked them away, but Sunny Eden was in top physical condition. Apparently her tear ducts worked just as well, or better, than everything else.

The blood drained from his face when he saw it—or, more accurately, when he didn't see it.

The motor home was gone. The space where it had been was just that—space. Empty, incredibly bleak-looking space.

Zack stared, feeling as though he'd been punched in the stomach.

Then his mind began to race. Propane. Motor homes needed propane. For hot water, for cooking, for all kinds of things. And she'd have to move the motor home to go get the propane.

He tried to hold that thought as he hurried up to the midway.

But when he got there, his hopes died a quick and painful death. Motor homes needed propane, but the Garden of Eden did not. Sunny's red trailer was gone, too. She had packed up her wares and run out on him. Run out on him and Cheryl and his mother, all the people who had come to care about her, without even an explanation or a decent goodbye.

Zack's gaze dropped to the dusty ground as he turned and walked in the direction of his car. His stomach was churning, but it was not with the pain of loss.

Whereas before, with the incident of Cheryl, he had felt nothing but compassion and concern for Sunny, now, with her cowardly departure, he felt nothing but disgust. She believed she had been the cause of a serious episode with a fifteen-year-old girl, and instead of facing what she considered to be a mistake and trying to make amends, she had turned and fled.

Sunny Eden, who preached to others about taking chances and taking responsibility for their lives, was totally gutless. And Zack could not respect that. Nor could he continue to care for someone he couldn't respect.

He reached his car and swung his long body inside. He jammed the car into reverse, then into gear, and gravel flew. He was better off without her, and so was Cheryl. He believed that now, but it didn't mean that learning it wasn't going to hurt for a while.

"Dr. Granger!" Cheryl's young face lit up when Zack walked into her hospital room. "Hi, I'm glad you came to visit. I'm climbing the walls in here. When are you going to let me out?"

Zack smiled, but it was a little forced. "In the morning, remember? I'm sure you're going to be just fine, but I want to keep an eye on you overnight just to be safe."

Cheryl rolled her eyes. "I think you're just getting desperate to fill up these empty beds. I hear business is a little slow right now."

"Thank heaven," Zack murmured dryly, and thought how much Cheryl had just sounded like Sunny. The empty-bed comment was just like something she'd come up with. He had Cheryl's chart in his hands. Needing something to do, he opened it and pretended to study it, even though he already knew by heart everything it said. "Yep, everything looks good to me." He closed the chart and looked at Cheryl. "Did they bring you your lunch earlier?"

She nodded. "Yeah, and it was great." She pulled a face. "Chicken broth, Jell-O, 7-Up—real healthy stuff."

Zack's smile was dry. "Cheryl, you haven't eaten anything solid in days. We're just trying to get your stomach ready for the real thing. If you started eating solid food right now, you'd probably. . . . Well, you'd probably lose it within five minutes."

"I know that," Cheryl said. "You can't just break a fast that quickly. But I'm talking about nutrition as opposed to junk food that isn't good for me. Now, what I'd like to have for dinner tonight is some vegetable broth—no meat now, just vegetable broth—and some fruit juice, fresh if possible, unsweetened, and an apple or something. I've read up on fasting, so I know how to do it. The only thing that went wrong was that I overdid on the exercise. I should have taken it easy, but I was so excited about the results I was getting, I guess I just got carried away.''

"I guess you did," he murmured, noting again how much she reminded him of Sunny.

It was amazing how much the girl had absorbed in just a few days. *But then again,* he thought, *look at how much I changed in just a few days. And my mother, and—* But he didn't want to think about that anymore. She was gone, and that was definitely for the best. Now he had to figure out how he was going to break it to Cheryl.

Within a matter of minutes, the girl was asking about Sunny, as Zack had known she would.

"So why isn't Sunny with you, Dr. Granger? Did she have to work?" Cheryl was putting on a cheerful face, but it was obvious that Sunny's absence was a disappointment. No doubt, she was more than a little hurt by it.

Zack ground his teeth and wondered again how Sunny could have run out on the girl without even a goodbye. She was just a kid, for heaven's sake. A kid who had idolized her and had had a very rough and scary day. She didn't deserve to be discarded this way. And neither did he.

But much as he wanted to, Zack couldn't bring himself to tell Cheryl how heartless and selfish her so-called friend had been. It would tear Cheryl's illusions to shreds, and as far as he was concerned, that could wait until morning.

"Yeah, I guess she felt like she couldn't do anything around here, so she might as well be trying to make some money." That explanation wasn't helping. Cheryl's blue eyes said so. Zack plunged on. "Besides, I told her you needed to rest. You don't need visitors tonight, you need sleep. Tomorrow you can do whatever you want. Tonight, I'm in charge."

"But Dr. Granger," Cheryl protested, "Jake's coming by tonight after work. You have to let him visit. And not just for a few minutes, either. I'm not kidding, Doctor, you have to let him visit."

At that moment, Zack Granger thanked God for Jake Scott. He pretended to mull it over. Then he smiled a benevolent smile. "Okay, Cheryl, you win. Jake can come and visit for a while, but only if you promise to rest in the meantime. And I mean it, no other visitors. Not even Sunny."

Cheryl grinned, sure that she'd won some big prize. "Okay. I promise. And, thanks."

"Sure. Oh, and I'll see what I can do about your dinner request, too."

Under the circumstances, it was the least he could do. The very least he could do to make up for Sunny Eden's desertion.

"She what?" Cheryl demanded the next morning. "What do you mean 'she's gone'? She can't be gone. The fair isn't even over yet."

Zack shrugged and sat down on the side of the bed. "I don't know what to tell you, Cheryl. She didn't talk to me, either, before she left. She just took off."

Cheryl's gaze dropped to her hands. "I see. Well, I guess she must have had her reasons." She bit her lip, remembering the scene with her mother.

Zack's jaw tightened. He could see the hurt behind Cheryl's blank expression. Damn Sunny! She had no right to have done this. "I guess she must have," he murmured. "Look, Cheryl, people are funny sometimes. And they're not perfect any of the time. Even Sunny."

Cheryl chuckled bitterly. "I sure thought she was perfect."

You and me both, kiddo, Zack thought. You and me both. But he said, "Maybe that was your mistake. We're walking in dangerous territory when we start idolizing human beings and turning them into gods. We're just asking to get hurt, because they're just like us—human—and they will make mistakes."

Cheryl nodded and looked up at him. "You know something? I thought she really liked me. I even thought that even if things didn't work out between you two and she didn't stay here in town, that we could still, you know, keep in touch." She looked down again and chuckled softly, tears beginning to brim on her dark lashes. "I thought we could write back and forth and call once in a while and...and I even thought maybe I could go visit her every now and then—you know, wherever she happened to be." She shook her head, hair hanging in her face.

There was a familiar slump to her shoulders that hadn't been there all week. It was the sight of that—that unconscious, I'm-worthless-and-I'd-like-to-be-invisible posture that got to Zack more than anything else. Sunny Eden, who had claimed to be so concerned about Cheryl's self-image, had dealt that image a monstrous blow. Cheryl, who needed so much to feel important and worthy, hadn't even rated a simple farewell.

Zack ground his teeth as fresh rage washed through him. Oh, yes, they were definitely better off without her, but that was no reason she should get off with this kind of thing scot-free. Before Sunny Eden left the state of Colorado, she was going to have a little souvenir to take with her—a piece of Zack's mind. Which was only fair, since she had already made off with a large chunk of his heart.

The late afternoon sun was dropping quickly, casting a watery-gold light and long shadows over the small campground. Travelers were pulling in in a steady stream, looking for a place to stop for the night. Sunny stepped wearily out of the motor home and dropped into a lounge chair. This had been one of the longest and loneliest days of her life.

She closed her eyes and rubbed her temple with her fingertips, trying to think. Had she made the right decision in leaving the way she had? Was there a better way to have handled it? Undoubtedly there was. She had just been too shaken up to figure it out at the time.

And now it was done.

By now Zack and Cheryl and Martha and everyone else knew she was gone. Without a word. Without an explanation. Without, as they would probably think, a backward glance.

If they only knew.

She blew out a sigh and dropped her head back, keeping her eyes closed. She didn't want to see the other campers around her. It was nearly dinnertime, and families and friends were lighting barbecue grills and camp stoves and making a royally festive occasion out of the meal. In the next campsite, dark-haired kids were helping to shuck corn so they could sink their little teeth into fresh corn on the cob.

In another site, a trio of children had just brought back small piles of kindling and firewood. After dark, there would be a campfire. But they didn't want to wait till after dark. Sunny would hear them asking yet again if they could roast the marshmallows yet.

"No," the mother snapped, impatient after so many requests. "And if you don't stop asking, you're not going to roast them at all!"

Sunny bit her lip, understanding the woman's impatience but wanting to caution her just the same. *Discipline them, Mommy, yes; they need you for that.*

But, oh, please, don't ever forget to appreciate them for what they are—children, in all their impatient, rambunctious, excitable glory....

"Well, if it isn't the voodoo queen," a male voice drawled. "Just relaxing and soaking up what's left of the afternoon sunshine?"

Sunny's eyes flew open in shock and alarm. Zack was standing there, silhouetted by the backdrop of sunlight. His face was in shadow, so she couldn't see his expression. But she didn't have to. She knew what those black eyes would contain.

She sat up quickly, her heart beating a mile a minute. "What are you doing here? How did you find me?"

He shrugged, an easy, nonchalant gesture that told her nothing. "Wasn't too hard. Pueblo's not a very big town. I checked the fairground first, but nothing's going on there yet. So I got a phone book and called the campgrounds."

He came a step closer. Sunny had to steel herself not to flinch. She put a hand up as a visor, knowing she had to see his face. But when she did, she was confused. There was a blankness to his expression that she hadn't expected. Actually, it was a blankness that went along quite well with his bland, nearly casual manner. It threw her completely off guard.

Why was he here?

Her eyes widened as a thought came to her. Had he come to get her? To tell her he didn't blame her and talk her into going back with him? Going home with him?

Her heart started racing so fast, she thought it might burst. Was it possible that Zack didn't blame her for Cheryl's illness? That he hadn't just reverted to his original opinions of her? *Was he here to say he still wanted her?*

She had to find out. After all, he had driven sixty miles to see her. Surely that must mean something.

Forcing an outward calmness, she eased herself out of the chair and stood up, moving to where she could see him without squinting into the sunlight.

She licked her lips. "I'm glad you came. I've been . . . regretting not talking to you before I left."

"Have you?" It was a low question that stirred her blood.

She nodded. "Mmm-hmm. I don't think that was really the way to handle the situation, but I wasn't thinking too clearly at the time. I just sort of . . . reacted." She took a step toward him and reached out a hand. "I'm sorry."

"Are you?" Instead of taking her hand, Zack folded his arms over his chest and leaned back on his heels.

Sunny swallowed and twisted her fingers together. A chill ran up her spine, leaving spreading goose bumps in its wake. This wasn't going the way she had begun to hope.

"Yes, I am. I should have...I should have said goodbye." But she wished desperately that there would never be a need for goodbyes between them. If only Zack would tell her that. But all he was doing was standing there, watching her with that blank look, making her crazy with his silence. "I should have also—"

Suddenly, something in him snapped. His hands dropped to his sides, and his dark eyes flashed.

"I'll tell you what you should have done," he snapped. "You should have been concerned about that fifteen-year-old girl! I obviously mean nothing to you, and that's okay—in fact that's just damned fine with me—but that girl thought you cared about her, Dr. Eden.

"There she was, lying in a hospital bed—which she reached, I might add, because she wanted so damned badly to be just like you—and you didn't even have the common decency to stick around and make sure she was going to be all right. Or at the very least, swing by there on your way out of town and out of her life to say goodbye!

"The rest of you might be healthy as hell, Doctor, but I think you ought to find yourself a good surgeon and see if he can come up with a way to give you a heart. I don't think I've ever seen anybody as cold inside as you are. And now that I have," he said in a low voice, "I do believe I've seen about as much as I can stomach."

Without another word, he turned and walked away.

It took Sunny a second to recover, then she was running after him. She couldn't let him leave. Not like this. Not at all.

She loved him. Lord, how she loved him. And she couldn't stand for him to go on thinking of her this way. She'd make him understand that she'd just been scared ... scared of just exactly what was happening now. Scared of losing him.

"Zack!" she called. "Wait!" She got to his car just as he was settling into the driver's seat. He paused, the door still open, and stared icily up at her.

"What?" he said.

"Let me explain." She pushed her hair back from her face. "I already told you that I regretted the way I handled things. I just ... couldn't think straight at the time. I—I just wish ..."

Zack shook his head. "Forget it, Doctor. I wish a lot of things, but in the end, it doesn't make a damn bit of difference, does it? What's done is done, and anybody who could do what you did to that kid is somebody I don't even want to waste time thinking about anymore. Now—" he grabbed the door handle and started to pull the door shut "—I've said what I came to say, so I guess I'll just be moseying along." He raised his right hand and tipped a pretend hat. "So long, Doctor. I can honestly say it's been hell knowing you."

The car door slammed.

Dr. Zachary Granger left.
Dr. Sunny Eden stood there and cried.
Again.
This just seemed to be the day for that sort of thing.

Chapter Nine

He was right, of course, Sunny thought as she maneuvered the motor home back out onto the dark highway. She had been wrong—absolutely, positively, totally *wrong* in the way she'd handled things. Good Lord, what had possessed her to act that way?

But she knew, oh, how she knew. It had been a terrible day, what with the Cheryl scare and facing her old hospital fears, and then Cheryl's mother blaming her and threatening to sue her and...

She shook her head to clear it. All that had been yesterday, and today...well, today, she definitely had some amends to make.

As she drove, she tried to figure out what she was going to tell Cheryl. The hour's drive passed all too

quickly, and by the time it was over and she was exit-
ing the freeway, the only solution she had come up
with was to tell the girl the truth. It was the only way
that everything really made sense. Cheryl would understand, she was sure. And Martha. Now, Zack, he
was a different story altogether.

She had already tried to explain it to him, and he
hadn't even bothered to listen. That hurt, but she did
understand where all that rage was coming from. He
had been right, and she had been wrong. Maybe her
coming back would help. He would see that she'd realized what needed to be done and had come back to
set things right.

She sighed and put Zack out of her mind. She
would have to think about him later. Right now, she
needed to find Cheryl. She stopped at a gas station and
went to the phone booth.

The phone book had a list of Evanses that looked a
half a mile long.

Sunny frowned, trying to remember if Cheryl had
ever mentioned her father's name. She remembered
her saying that he was a salesman and that he was out
of town a lot and that they really weren't very
close...but, no, Sunny didn't believe the girl had ever
mentioned his first name. Terrific.

So she had two choices. She could get a bucket of
change and call every Evans in the book, or she could
call Zack.

Or, she realized, brightening suddenly, she could call Zack's mother. Yes, that was it, she decided, thumbing through the white pages. She would call Zack's mother.

A weary-sounding male voice answered the telephone. Sunny bit her lip, knowing she had put the tiredness into Zack's voice. There was a sharp, strong desire to try to talk to him again, explain herself, but no words came.

Instead, she swallowed quickly and switched to plan B—the one she'd had in mind for just this occasion.

"Hello," she said, speaking through her nose in a high voice that Zack would never recognize. "May I speak with Martha, please?"

"I'm sorry," Zack said. "She can't come to the phone right now. May I take a message?"

Sunny frowned, thrown off guard. "No, thank you—well, wait, maybe you can. I'm a friend of Martha's. Do you have any idea when she could return my call?"

There was a tired sigh, and Sunny ached all over. She knew how Zack felt. "Probably ten, fifteen minutes," he said. "Do you want her to call?"

"Yes," Sunny decided. "The number is..." She had to scrape something brown and sticky off the pay phone to see the number. She read it to Zack, then tried to get off the phone quickly. "Thank you very much. I'll be waiting to hear from her." She hung up the phone.

The pay phone rang, and Sunny nearly jumped out of her skin. "Hello, Martha? This is Sunny. Listen, I—" She stopped, realizing she hadn't given the woman a chance to speak. It could be anybody on the other end, even a wrong number. "Martha? This is you, isn't it?"

There was silence on the line. Sunny's face fell. It was only in that instant that she realized how much she'd been looking forward to talking to the older woman—and not just about Cheryl, either. She suddenly found herself wanting to spill out everything to her.

"What do you want?" It was a flat, hard voice. Zack's voice.

Sunny faltered. The last thing she would have expected was for him to call back. "Zack, hi. I guess you recognized my voice?" Hope sang through her. Maybe he had called because he wanted to talk, wanted to hear her side.

"No, no I didn't. I just thought you sounded so weird, maybe I'd better try to find out what this was all about." There was a short silence. "So, what is this all about?"

"Well," Sunny said, feeling ridiculous about trying to hide who she was. "It's about Cheryl," she explained, focusing back to the original purpose of the call.

"What about Cheryl?" There was an added alertness to his voice, concern for the girl.

"Well, I was just trying to find out how to get hold of her. There are so many Evanses in the book, and I figured your mother would know her father's name, and—" She stopped herself, took a breath and went on. "So anyway, I'm sure you can help me."

"I'm sure I can't."

The flat, hard statement took Sunny by surprise. "You mean you won't," she accused, anger flaring.

"That's right, Ms. Eden, I won't. I don't know what you came back here for, but you wasted a trip. The last thing Cheryl needs is for you to come back into her life and—"

"Wait just a minute, Dr. Granger!" Sunny snapped. "Who are you to decide who Cheryl—or your mother, for that matter—can talk to? And besides, *Dr.* Granger, you're the one who drove clear over to Pueblo to tell me that I should have talked to everyone—especially Cheryl—to begin with. So what? You think that just because it's been a day, the damage is done and can't be fixed? You think that just because I made a mistake, no one will let me rectify it?

"Well, let me tell *you* something, Dr. Granger. I think—no, I know—you're wrong. Everybody in this world isn't as narrow-minded and unforgiving as you are! *Some* people would give me a chance to explain! Some—"

"You don't have a good enough excuse for what you did yesterday," Zack said.

"Fine," Sunny said, eyes threatening to fill up again. "You've made your position quite clear. But like I said, there are others who will be more understanding. Now, if you don't mind, I'd like to talk to your mother, please."

"She doesn't want to talk to you."

Sunny pressed her lips together. "Well, maybe that's true and maybe it isn't. Past history has taught me not to take your word as fact." She remembered the first time she'd met him, when he'd returned Martha's vitamins. Was that only less than a week ago? And their night on the midway. Was that really just a few days ago? It all seemed like another lifetime.

She blew out a sigh and felt very very tired. "Look, Doctor, I don't want to argue with you. If your mother really doesn't want to talk to me, that's fine, and I guess maybe I can understand. But I want to hear it from her. And as far as Cheryl goes, I think that if you put your own prejudices aside for a few minutes, you'll have to agree that my talking to her is a whole lot kinder for her than if I never contact her again. You said so yourself, remember?"

Silence.

Then Zack sighed, too. "Okay. You win. But I hope to God you handle this right. You've caused enough trouble around here, Dr. Eden."

He gave her Cheryl's father's name and the address, which Sunny jotted down on a piece of scrap paper.

"Thank you, Doctor," she said evenly. "Now, about your mother..."

"My mother is in the shower. If you're going to be hanging around there, I'll give her your message. But I have no idea how long it's going to be."

"I'm not positive how long I'll be here, either. It depends on what happens with Cheryl. Give your mother my message, and, if you would, tell her that if I'm not here, I'll call her tomorrow. I'd like to see her before I leave town again."

"Tomorrow?" It was a wary sound. "You're staying in town then?"

"Yes," Sunny said. "At least long enough to get my mess cleaned up."

A silence that was long and full of too many feelings crackled over the telephone lines.

Sunny spoke first. "I'll hang up now." She hesitated. "And Zack—thanks for Cheryl's address and giving your mother my message."

"Sure."

"Well..."

Silence.

"Bye," she said, and hung up the phone.

Zack was slow to replace the receiver. He stood staring at it for a long time.

"So, you see, Cheryl, a lot of things contributed to the way I acted yesterday. My husband had died in a hospital, and I was reliving all that, and I was so afraid that you were really sick, too. I just didn't deal with it very well. And then, when I—" Sunny paused and took a deep breath "—when I heard that you'd been living on nothing but vitamins—vitamins that I sold you—I felt like it was all my fault and—"

"But it wasn't!" Cheryl said earnestly.

They had met at a little pizza joint. It was buzzing with high-school kids, but they had found a corner booth that afforded a degree of privacy. Thankfully, Cheryl's mother had been out.

"It wasn't your fault at all," Cheryl insisted. "You didn't tell me not to eat."

"But I should have noticed the signs of starvation," Sunny said wryly. "Nobody loses weight the way you did without starving themselves."

Cheryl shook her head. "That's dumb, Sunny. If you want to use that reason to blame someone, then you could blame anybody who saw me—my parents, Jake, even Dr. Granger. He noticed I was looking different, but he didn't figure it out, either."

Sunny tipped her head to the side. "I hadn't thought about that," she admitted, recognizing the truth of it. If anyone was going to notice something, it should have been the girl's mother. Or even Zack. He was a doctor, after all. So how could he blame her...?

She frowned suddenly as a new thought hit her. Actually, she wasn't at all sure that he did blame her for that. All he'd really talked about was the way she'd run out on everybody.

"Besides," Cheryl continued, "it isn't anybody's fault except mine. I mean, I just tried to do too much too fast. But you know, I'm not really sorry. I mean, for the first time in my life, I really did something, you know? I gave it everything I've got. Maybe I made a couple of mistakes with it, but I did it. I've never really succeeded with anything before. Now I feel like I can do anything."

"You look like you can do anything," Sunny said, beginning to feel warm all over. Apparently some good had come out of the situation after all. Feeling better than she'd felt in two days, Sunny relaxed against the back of the seat. This was nice, sitting here talking to Cheryl. She wished she didn't have to leave.

But living in the same town with Zachary Granger would be sheer hell. After she straightened things out with Martha, she'd be on her way back to Pueblo. And after that? Well, after that, she didn't really know, and she didn't really care.

She had done too much caring in the last week, and the truth was, she was out of practice for this sort of thing. When you cared deeply, you hurt deeply. She had already learned that lesson once in her life. She only wished she hadn't had to learn it twice. And she promised herself that she would never let herself find out whether or not the third time really was the charm.

Cheryl had been a little wary, a little reserved, when Sunny first called her on the phone. The same could definitely not be said for Martha Granger. Sunny could have hugged the woman when she heard her warm, ever-friendly voice come over the lines.

"Sunny! I've been waiting all morning to hear from you. Zack gave me your message, and I tried to call so many times that old Jonathan at the filling station finally came out and answered the pay phone! So how are you, my girl?"

Sunny laughed, warmed to her toes. She loved this woman. "I'm fine, Martha, just fine. A whole lot better than I was the day before yesterday. Listen, I wondered if maybe we could have brunch together or something. I...sort of wanted to explain why I ran out on everybody the other day."

"You don't have to explain anything to me," Martha said. "You had had one stinker of a day. I tried to tell Zack that, but you know how stubborn he can be. Although, I have to admit I've never known him to just keep on holding a grudge after somebody apologizes. He's usually a lot more understanding than that."

"Oh, well," Sunny said, trying to pretend that Zachary Granger's understanding didn't matter. "I guess there's an exception to every rule."

There was a brief, thoughtful silence. Then Martha was back, bright and perky as before. "Anyway, I'd dearly love to have brunch with you. Where and when?"

They settled the details. Sunny was smiling faintly as she hung up the phone.

Martha dressed quickly, then headed down the hall to Zack's office. Sherry, Zack's receptionist, looked up with a smile.

"How are you this morning, Martha?"

"Fine, just fine. Is the good doctor busy?"

"He's between patients. He had me reschedule everybody who wasn't urgent. He's in his office. You want me to buzz him?"

Martha shook her head. "No, thanks. I'll just knock on my way in." She started to leave, then paused thoughtfully. "He had you reschedule his patients, huh?"

"Yes. Today, yesterday, the day before . . ."

"Did he say why?" But Martha knew. A small smile of satisfaction tugged at her lips.

"Nope. Just said something about his bedside manner stinking right now—his words, not mine. But to tell you the truth, I think his words were pretty apt."

"I know." Martha chuckled. "He hasn't exactly been a joy to have around the house lately, either. But chin up, Sherry. Things are going to get better. I think his life's going to be a little more . . . sunny from now on."

She was chuckling at her little pun as she walked down the hall. She had known Sunny wasn't the type to just leave without a word. She had merely been trying to cope with a difficult situation. And Zack was wrong about her. Martha had known that, too. It wasn't that Sunny didn't care. It was that she cared maybe a little too much—about Cheryl, about Martha herself and especially about Zack and Zack's opinion of her.

If he couldn't see that now, he would in time. Martha only hoped it didn't take too much time. After all, she didn't know how long she could get the future mother of her grandchildren—Zack's words, not hers—to stick around.

"I'm going to brunch," she announced to her son. "With Sunny."

Zack scowled. He had been expecting as much. "I guess if your time is worth so little to you, you might as well fritter it away." He waved a hand through the air to punctuate his statement.

Martha smiled, tender pangs tugging at her heart. Her son looked rough these days. His dark eyes were bloodshot from too little sleep, and his face looked haggard. For an instant she felt like a traitor. What kind of mother would consort with the person who had caused her child such pain? But the guilt passed quickly. Sunny might have acted in a way that had hurt him, but Zack could have tried to see her side of things, too.

After all, people made mistakes, acted foolishly. That was the nature of the human animal. Lord knew, she and Doc had had plenty of misunderstandings themselves, and they had both had their feelings hurt plenty of times. But in the end, love always won out over pride or pain or embarrassment.

In Martha's opinion, if Zachary refused to get beyond this and allowed the woman he loved to walk out of his life, well then, maybe he didn't deserve to have her at all. Love was a battle all the way through—acquiring it, admitting it, keeping it going. But oh, it was worth the fight.

She tipped her head to the side, challenging her son with a twinkling glance. "Is there anything you'd like me to tell her for you?"

Zack leaned back in his swivel chair and studied her through narrowed eyes. "Yeah, you can tell her to go straight to—"

"Zachary!" Martha snapped, then turned on her heel. Obviously Zack was in no reasonable frame of mind as yet. Quite obviously.

She left and closed the door behind her, leaving her only son to sit and stew, knowing this was all hard for him, but also knowing it was part of the process of working through.

Brunch was wonderful, with lots of laughter and warm moments. For the first time since Dan's death, Sunny fully explained her past and how Cheryl's illness had reopened that wound. Martha listened sympathetically, able to understand Sunny's loss. Then, gently, the conversation eased over to the present.

Their conversation from then on was light and happy, and the only shadow on the visit was when Martha mentioned Zack. Sunny's face clouded visibly, but she tried to cover with a falsely bright smile.

"How is Zack, anyway?"

"Stubborn," Martha said. "Like I told you on the phone." She dabbed at her mouth with her napkin. "But he'll come around, don't you worry."

"Come around to what?" Sunny asked, then decided it was pointless to play dumb. She shook her head. "I don't think so, Martha. He just wants to forget he ever met me. And maybe that's just as well after all."

"Nonsense!" Martha snorted. "He might want to right now, but I'll guarantee you he'll never be able to do it. He's never fallen for anyone like he fell for you."

Sunny pulled a wry face.

"No, really," Martha said. "I was beginning to wonder if he'd ever find anybody to settle down with.

Then when you came along..." She rolled her eyes. "Like I said, don't worry about it, he'll come around. It just might take a little time. He fell for you hard, so I think he really felt it when he thought he'd lost you. Finding out just how much he cared probably scared him to death."

Sunny smiled at the woman's optimism. She only wished she could feel the same assurance that it would all work out in the end. Maybe Martha was right. After all, she was his mother. Maybe she knew her son well enough to know... Sunny gave herself a mental shake.

The future would hold whatever it would hold. She supposed she'd just have to wait to find out. And try, in the meantime, not to think about what might have been.

Chapter Ten

The days dragged on. The Pueblo fair was coming to an end. Every day Sunny had gone to her booth with the hope that that day she would see a familiar face, a well-known dark head, in the crowd. And every day, another piece of her died a little.

On Saturday night, the last night of the fair, Sunny dragged herself back from dinner and set up her display of wares. She wore white jeans and a scarlet shell sweater. Her uniform had been retired, along with her crowd-summoning spiel. Somewhere between the dangerous situation with Cheryl and her problems with Zack, her enthusiasm for her work had gone right down the drain.

Now, instead of providing encouragement and entertainment, she simply sat there and sold vitamins. When people asked advice, she pointed to relevant pamphlets, but was careful not to offer any personal suggestions. After all, she was not a doctor. The information was available, and people could read it all and then decide for themselves. Besides, who was she to give advice on anything?

She had made a total wreck of her own life, and her health wasn't exactly anything to brag about these days, either. She had stopped running, partly because of the bittersweet memories of the last time she'd run and partly because she just didn't seem to have the energy to do it. And her diet—well, that had really become a disgrace.

Last night she had even had a whole stick of cotton candy, just gobbled it down without even tasting it. It hadn't even fazed her. That was the thing. Nothing seemed to faze her anymore—not people, not their problems, nothing. She felt like an automaton and acted accordingly.

"Excuse me, Dr. Eden, but I've run out of a few things, and I need to stock up."

Sunny's eyes brightened as she looked up to see two of her favorite people in the world. "Martha, Cheryl! What are you guys doing here?" Automatically her gaze slid beyond them, looking for a third musketeer. There was none.

Martha saw Sunny's searching glance and felt a stab of sympathy. No, Zack had not come, even though he had been strongly invited. She had told him that tonight was the last night of the Pueblo fair and reminded him that Sunny would be out of the state tomorrow, headed to Kansas and then the rest of the Midwest. Zack had said that was good. Oh, yes, and "have a good time," he had said that, too, while Martha had stood there, wanting to shake him.

She had been so sure that he'd come to his senses during this long week and go after Sunny. But apparently she had been wrong. Dead wrong. And she felt so guilty for her part in assuring Sunny and making the separation just that much worse by offering hope and dragging the whole thing out. Now it was her bitterly awful duty to put Sunny's mind to rest. Time to quit thinking about Zack and get on with her life. Blast it all anyway!

She pasted on a smile. "We knew this was your last night in the area, so we thought we'd come and take you out on the town. That is, if you can get away from work for a little bit?"

Sunny shrugged. "Sure. I'm not doing much business these days, anyway. Just give me a minute to close up shop."

Cheryl and Martha jumped in to help, and the table was cleared and the trailer locked tight in record time.

"Well," Sunny said with forced brightness. "What shall we do, ladies?"

"Well..." Cheryl drawled, tipping her head to the side. "We could go look for some men...."

"Cheryl!" Sunny glanced at Martha. "You don't just go looking for men."

"Sure you do," Cheryl said. "I mean, that's what half the people come to the fair for—to meet people. It's very romantic to do the midway with a perfect stranger."

Sunny pressed her lips together, remembering just how romantic it could indeed be. After all, Zack had basically been a stranger. Perfect? Maybe not. But that had been one of the most magical nights of her life. And the last thing she wanted to do was attempt to copy it by picking up some strange guy.

"I really don't think—" She glanced to Martha for help, but the older woman seemed to be thinking along different lines.

"I don't know, Sunny," Martha said. "It might be fun. I mean, you know, if we just happened to meet someone interesting, I don't think *I* would object to a little innocent fun at the fair."

Sunny frowned. "I thought you guys came here to see me?" After all, she thought, this was the last night they'd have to be together for a long time—maybe ever.

"We did." Cheryl nodded, then slid a sly look at Martha. "It's just that on the way in, we met these two guys. I think they must have been grandfather and grandson or something. And they asked us if we'd like to join them.''

Sunny lowered her gaze so they wouldn't see the hurt in her eyes. "I see," she murmured. "Well, that sounds like fun. Why don't you two go with them for a while, and we'll visit a little bit before you go home."

"Oh, we're not going home," Cheryl said.

"No, we decided we'd probably have a late night, so we're just going to get a room," Martha added.

"Oh, stay with me!" Sunny brightened. Even if they did go off gallivanting, they could stay up late and talk. Besides, the motor home, for one night at least, would not remind her of a coffin—close, dark, suffocatingly silent. "I have plenty of room. It'll sleep six easily."

Cheryl and Martha exchanged glances. "We'd love to stay with you," Martha said. "But on one condition. That you come and join us on the midway."

"Join who?" she asked, but knowing what the answer would be.

"Us," Martha said. "And Rex and Jeff."

"You already know their names?"

"Sure," Cheryl nodded. "You don't think we'd go off with complete strangers, do you?"

At Sunny's consternation, Martha and Cheryl laughed.

"I'd better explain," Martha said. "Rex—that's Jeff's grandfather—is a widower. He and I went to school together years and years ago. We ran into them near the front gate. Now, we don't really have to go with them tonight, but, well, to tell you the truth, it's been six years since I've been with a man on anything that resembled a date, and, to be perfectly honest, I think it's high time. Don't you?''

Sunny blinked, her thoughts automatically going to what Zack would think about his mother dating. Then she nodded vigorously and took a deep breath. ''Martha, I think that sounds terrific. I'm happy for you.''

''But we're not going if you don't come, too,'' Cheryl said.

''But I'd be a fifth wheel. I wouldn't even—''

Cheryl looked at Martha. ''You'd better tell her the rest.

Martha nodded. ''Yes, I guess I'd better. When we told Rex there were three of us, he rounded up one of his son's single friends. He knows practically everybody that walks by. And his friend is—well, Cheryl, what did you think of Chris?''

Cheryl rolled her eyes. ''I think I wish I was a few years older.''

Sunny frowned. ''Hey, what happened to Jake?''

''Nothing.'' Cheryl shrugged but lowered her eyes. Sunny began to get the feeling that all was not as it seemed. As Cheryl went on with a rather feeble explanation about not wanting to be tied down, and being able to date more than one person, Sunny's feeling of unease grew and grew. Something was going on here, but she couldn't quite figure out what.

When she finally agreed to go along with the plans for the other women's sakes, she thought they seemed just a little too relieved. A little too grateful to make much sense at all, in fact. There was a small frown on Sunny's brow as she trailed along after Martha and Cheryl, listening to what seemed to be the senseless chatter of extremely forced gaiety. What was going on?

But by the time an hour or so had passed, Sunny had the puzzle worked out. It was so obvious, it was almost laughable, in a sad sort of way. Zack didn't want her, and the two women had obviously finally come to an acceptance of the fact. So in fixing her up with Chris Temple, they were trying to help her get on with things.

There was something very final about it all.

Whereas Sunny had thought her relationship with Zack over and done with a week ago, there was just something different about his mother trying so hard to matchmake. Her efforts to cheer had the totally opposite effect. As Martha elbowed her and asked what she thought of Chris, Sunny felt like she wanted to throw up. If not even Martha believed anymore, it was really and truly over. Definitely, positively, unequivocally over.

"Excuse me," she said, fighting to control the rolling of her stomach. "I'm really not feeling very well." She stepped backward, away from the group, away from the reality Martha presented. "I think I need to go and lie down for a while."

"I'll walk you home," Chris offered, extending a hand. Tall and blond, with a beautiful tan, the man was more than handsome, he was like some golden god. Yet he didn't seem in the least conceited. Or dumb, as fabulous-looking men sometimes were. As far as Sunny had been able to tell, he was great all the way around—interesting and interested in others, intelligent, funny...perfect.

But he wasn't Zack. It was just that simple. And she wasn't interested.

"No. No, thank you, Chris, really. I'm sorry to have to run out on you all like this, but—" Her stomach rolled again, seriously warning her to get away. "I really have to go." She looked at Martha and Cheryl. "You two come back to the camper when you're done. Don't you dare get a room."

She turned and fled, this time welcoming the dark, which tonight seemed to hold the promise of a healing, the hint that it was finally time to mourn the past once and for all, to feel every single bit of the pain and then put it behind her so she could begin to rebuild her future, something she'd done once and would now have to do all over again.

It was August, and it was hot. The Missouri county fairgoers wore shorts and T-shirts and sandals. Sunny had started wearing her summer costume three weeks ago—star-spangled blue-and-white shorts, a white short-sleeved cotton blouse, red suspenders and, as always, her colorful top hat.

She was doing well, selling more than ever, and feeling pretty good, too. Except, of course, for the empty hollowness that had made a home in the pit of her stomach. She lived with that, yes, as she had after Dan died, but even that was beginning to shrink.

It would take time, she knew. Healing and recovering from loss always did. But, as she had learned from the past, she was a survivor—no, she was a winner, as all human beings inherently were. And she intended to do her best to practice what she preached.

Of course, that didn't stop her from thinking about Zack, or dreaming about him, any more than Dan's death had stopped her from remembering him for the past three years. But... Onward, Sunny told herself as she climbed up onto the small stage she had had built for her presentation.

She picked up her microphone and went to work.

"Step right up, folks, now don't be shy. I've come all the way from Los Angeles, California, to let all you nice folks in the State of Missouri in on a little secret of mine. No, actually, it's a big secret..."

The secret that, yes, there truly was life after death—many kinds of death, and you just had to find a way to go on.

Zack leaned casually against the edge of the Sno-Cone Shack, his dark eyes watching Sunny intently. He could barely stand it. There she was, in the flesh, not a hundred yards away. After three-and-a-half weeks, there she finally was.

The sight of her was nearly killing him with wanting, with regret, with fear and with love so great and strong it would never go away.

That, he knew. With or without her in his life, the way he felt about her was never going to go away. He had just spent the most miserable, stinking, *rotten* month of his life. And he knew that it had been self-induced.

In the beginning he had been kidding himself. It wasn't Sunny or anything she had ever said or done that had kept them apart. It was him, pure and simple. It was the way he'd felt when she'd left town and gone to Pueblo. Good God in Heaven, he had had a taste of what it would be like if they got even more involved and then she left him. And it had scared him half to death.

Still leaning against the metal Sno-Cone Shack, Zack twisted his mouth wryly. He had accused Sunny of having no guts. But didn't they say that preachers usually preached most loudly and most often about their own sins and weaknesses? He had been one hell of a sinning, self-righteous, gutless preacher. And Sunny had been his poor, unsuspecting flock of one.

Thank God she seemed to be doing better than he was. She looked great, she was working as well or better than ever, she—

Zack stopped his rambling thoughts and pulled himself up straight. *Quit stalling, Granger,* he told himself. *You want to talk about guts? Get your tail up there and see if you've really got guts. See if you've got the backbone to walk up there and let her slap you down in front of fifty-some people.* Because that would be justice, Zack knew.

After the way he'd treated her, he wouldn't blame her if she spat in his face. His mother had finally told him about Sunny's late husband, after putting up with his growling for two weeks. It explained so much to him. But then, he had realized that the only thing that had come between them was himself. It didn't matter if Sunny never told him about her painful past; she had come to grips with it. What mattered was their future. As he approached the gathering crowd, he prayed that she'd give him another chance.

"My friends," Sunny began, getting into her spiel. It felt good to be working well again, to have all her old enthusiasm back. True, since her experience with Cheryl, she was a tad more careful about her advice, but she did so strongly believe in what she was doing. She put one hand to the brim of her top hat and looked down at the small crowd gathered at her feet.

"I am here today to tell you that things can change. From this moment on, you can be a new person—I *guarantee* it. Right here, in my Garden of Eden, you find the fountain of youth! I said, you can *find* the *fountain* of *youth!* Do I hear a 'hallelujah' for an announcement like that?"

Sunny lifted her eyebrows and looked expectantly at her audience. When there was no response, she frowned, narrowed her eyes and cupped a hand to her ear.

"Say 'hallelujah,'" she demanded, whipping the rolled sheet of paper from her shorts pocket and snapping it open. "See? It's right here, in the script. 'The crowd says "hallelujah." That's what it says, right after I tell you about the fountain of youth. Now, are you all going to do your part or not?"

The audience relaxed into chuckles.

"Hallelujah! The fountain of youth," one male voice said.

Sunny nodded and smiled. "That's better," she said, and started to reroll the script. "Now, where was I?" It was then that she faltered in the pitch she'd given hundreds of times.

Her green eyes widened and flew to search the crowd. There had been something so hauntingly, achingly familiar in that male voice. Something so... But that was crazy. Zack was hundreds of miles away. And even if he was only a hundred feet away, he wouldn't cross the street to see her.

She cleared her throat, and her mind scrambled to regain her place in her speech. Where was she? She touched her hand to her cheek and realized she was shaking. She had to pull herself together.

"Now," she said again, but without her former force. "Where was I?"

"You were about to tell us about the fountain of youth."

There it was again. That voice! Sunny shaded her eyes and scanned the crowd, but she couldn't find the man belonging to that treacherously familiar voice. It couldn't be Zack, but the very thought of him was throwing her so off balance, she wasn't sure she could finish her pitch.

She took a deep breath and tried to go on. "Yes, the fountain of youth...uh..." What about the fountain of youth? her mind screamed.

"Yeah, the fountain of youth." The voice was closer this time, but off to the side.

Sunny caught a glimpse of a dark head moving through the crowd. But, of course, it couldn't be...

"You know, that thing that makes you feel great," the voice said, and a man—a dark-haired, very handsome man by the name of Zachary Granger—was climbing up the side steps to join her on her small stage. "That thing that makes you feel like you can do great things and conquer the world. That thing that makes you remember to have more questions than answers.... That thing that you know you can't live without...."

He was standing beside her, melting her with his dark eyes. He looked older, the grooves around his mouth deeper and more noticeable than they had been in that other lifetime. But what Sunny really saw was in his eyes; they told her most of what she needed to know. He loved her—beyond measure.

The emotion in him was raw and showing in front of a whole crowd of people, and he didn't care. Any warning that might normally have come to her upon seeing him again went right down the tubes when she saw all that. Zack would never reject her again. Like her, he had obviously had his own ghosts to battle, and like her, he had won.

"Zack," she breathed, unable to take her eyes from his face.

But instead of holding her gaze, he turned to face the crowd. "Folks, I want to tell you something about the fountain of youth. For me, this woman is that wondrous thing we've been telling you about. She's my life, she's my blood, she's my vitality. I've been without her for the past month, and I've been dying because of it. I'm here to beg her forgiveness and ask her to marry me and fill me up again and again and again . . . as long as we both shall live."

And he turned toward her, hands and arms itching and burning to touch her, but knowing that she had to make the first move. If she told him to leave, he would. He owed her that.

The crowd waited with bated breath.

Sunny stood there, letting it all sink in, wondering if this was just one more of a thousand dreams.

And then she fell into his waiting arms.

The kiss was long and tender, charged with chemistry and hot emotion. Their lips met while their too-long-empty arms rediscovered the joy of being filled. His mouth grazed her cheek, her neck, pressing hotly along the tantalizing path it chose, and Sunny tipped her head back to grant access. This moment she would grant him anything he wanted. In the back of her mind was the knowledge that there would be talking, explaining to do later, on both sides. But all that was mere formality.

Here and now was what mattered. The feel, the smell, the taste of him—that was reality. There was a singing in her veins and a thundering in her ears . . .

A thundering in her ears that sounded like . . . applause.

They both seemed to realize it at the same moment and reluctantly but quickly broke apart. Their smiles were sheepish and their faces flushed as they faced the applauding crowd.

Zack bowed to the audience rather elegantly. "Thank you, thank you very much," he said, and turned to Sunny. "And thank you, thank *you* very much, Dr. Eden."

Sunny's smile was both radiant and tender. "Any time, Dr. Granger. Any time."

Later, much later, Zack and Sunny fixed a cozy dinner in the motor home. Over candlelight, they toasted each other with stemmed glasses of sparkling mineral water.

"To you," Zack said. "My light, my love, my life."

"To us," Sunny said. "And our future together."

"Speaking of which..." Zack set his glass aside. "I need to ask you. Will it bother you very much, giving up your work?"

Sunny raised her eyebrows. "I didn't know I *would* be giving up my work. It seems to me I remember you saying something about my joining your practice at one time. Or was that all just talk?"

Zack shook his head quickly. "No, no, not at all. I meant that, then and now. I was just talking about giving up the traveling, the crowds, the showmanship that you're so good at."

Sunny shrugged. "I suppose I will miss that part of it to a degree. But then, I never planned on traveling with a carnival forever. Besides, I want my kids to have roots."

"Our kids," Zack said, and took a drink of the water. "You know, you're so good at what you can do with a crowd, and you're so good at inspiring people to better their lives, I just hate to think of you giving it up."

Sunny frowned. "Well, that may be, Dr. Granger, but I am not going to carry on this—" she stumbled over the word, but when it came past her lips, it felt wonderful "—this marriage of ours by mail. If you want me, you're going to get me full time."

Zack lifted his hands, palms up. "Of course, of course, Dr. Eden. I wouldn't have it any other way." He took her hand across the table and absently stroked it with his thumb. "While we were ... separated, I thought a lot about what our life together could be like, and I had an idea. That is, if you still want to work."

"Sure. What's the idea?"

"Well, an old school friend of mine is in television in Denver. I called him up one day and talked to him about the possibility of a local talk show. You know, one of those deals where everything's geared to solving problems and uplifting people, etcetera, etcetera."

"Yes," Sunny said warily. Was he really thinking what she thought he was thinking? Good heavens, she wasn't the television type! But it did warm her to her toes to think that Zack thought so much of her talents and her work.

"Well, I told Sam that I thought I knew the perfect host for that kind of show, someone who could entertain and encourage and still keep things upbeat and fun."

"And..."

"And," Zack said, looking smugly satisfied, "he's interested in talking more about it. He wants to meet with you and hear your ideas."

Sunny gaped. "But I don't have any ideas!"

His smile was crooked and dazzling. "You will," he said with great confidence. "Before we get back to Crystal Springs, you will."

And the more Sunny thought about it, the more certain she was that she would indeed have a few ideas. More than a few, she amended, as thoughts and visions came flying into her head. Just think, her mind said, of all the people you could reach via television....

"Hey, whoa," Zack said with a laugh. "Save the brainstorming for tomorrow. Tonight we have other things to discuss."

Sunny laughed. "You're right, we do." Her fingers closed more tightly over his. She still couldn't quite believe he was really here. Really hers. Forever.

"Such as," Zack said, giving her an exasperated look, "what we're going to do about my mother."

Her eyes widened. "What about her? How is she?"

He sighed heavily. "She's incorrigible, that's how she is. She thinks she's a teenager or something. Stays out half the night with this Rex character, never tells me where she's going or when she's going to be in, never—''

Sunny laughed. ''I think your mother is going to be very happy to hear that we're back together, Zack. If not for our sakes, then for hers. Once we're home, I'll do my level best to keep your mind so occupied, you won't have time to worry about your mother's affairs.''

Zack groaned. '''Affairs,' huh? Now that was a poor choice of words.''

''Oh, really?'' Sunny murmured. ''I think it was a fine choice of words.'' She got up and moved to his side of the table and sat on his lap. ''And trust me, Doctor, you're going to get a lot more satisfaction out of worrying about your own affairs from now on. I seem to recall you challenging a statement I made a while back....''

''Yeah?'' He nuzzled her ear. ''What statement was that?''

''I told you that I didn't think there was enough excitement in this world to satisfy me.''

''And?''

''And you said something to the effect that we'd have to see about that.''

''I did.''

''You did.''

"Then," Zack said, fitting her more comfortably to him, "I guess that's just exactly what we'll have to do."

Then his mouth covered hers as a beginning, a rather wonderful beginning, to fulfillment of that promise.

*   *   *   *   *

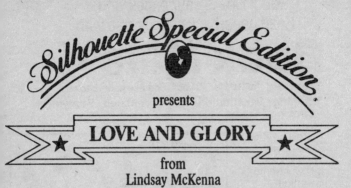

Silhouette Special Edition

presents

★ LOVE AND GLORY ★

from
Lindsay McKenna

Introducing a gripping new series celebrating our men—and women—in uniform. Meet the Trayherns, a military family as proud and colorful as the American flag, a family fighting the shadow of dishonor, a family determined to triumph—with **LOVE AND GLORY!**

June: **A QUESTION OF HONOR** (SE #529) leads the fast-paced excitement. When Coast Guard officer Noah Trayhern offers Kit Anderson a safe house, he unwittingly endangers his own guarded emotions.

July: **NO SURRENDER** (SE #535) Navy pilot Alyssa Trayhern's assignment with arrogant jet jockey Clay Cantrell threatens her career—and her heart—with a crash landing!

August: **RETURN OF A HERO** (SE #541) Strike up the band to welcome home a man whose top-secret reappearance will make headline news . . . with a delicate, daring woman by his side.

Three courageous siblings—
three consecutive months of

★ LOVE AND GLORY ★

Premiering in **June**, only in
Silhouette Special Edition.

You'll flip . . . your pages won't!
Read paperbacks *hands-free* with

Book Mate · I

The perfect "mate" for all your romance paperbacks

Traveling • Vacationing • At Work • In Bed • Studying • Cooking • Eating

Perfect size for all standard paperbacks, this wonderful invention makes reading a pure pleasure! Ingenious design holds paperback books OPEN and FLAT so even wind can't ruffle pages — leaves your hands free to do other things. Reinforced, wipe-clean vinyl-covered holder flexes to let you turn pages without undoing the strap . . . supports paperbacks so well, they have the strength of hardcovers!

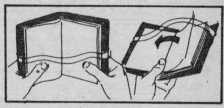

Pages turn WITHOUT opening the strap.

SEE-THROUGH STRAP

Reinforced back stays flat.

Built in bookmark.

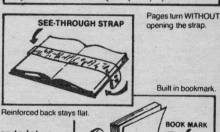

BOOK MARK

BACK COVER HOLDING STRIP

10" x 7¼", opened.
Snaps closed for easy carrying, too.

Available now. Send your name, address, and zip code, along with a check or money order for just $5.95 + .75¢ for postage & handling (for a total of $6.70) payable to Reader Service to:

Reader Service
Bookmate Offer
901 Fuhrmann Blvd.
P.O. Box 1396
Buffalo, N.Y. 14269-1396

Offer not available in Canada
*New York and Iowa residents add appropriate sales tax.

BM-G

FOUR UNIQUE SERIES
FOR EVERY WOMAN YOU ARE . . .

Silhouette Romance

Love, at its most tender, provocative,
emotional . . . in stories that will make you laugh and
cry while bringing you the magic of falling in love.

6 titles
per month

Silhouette Special Edition

Sophisticated, substantial and packed with
emotion, these powerful novels of life and love will
capture your imagination and steal your heart.

6 titles
per month

Silhouette Desire

Open the door to romance and passion. Humorous,
emotional, compelling—yet always a believable
and sensuous story—Silhouette Desire never
fails to deliver on the promise of love.

6 titles
per month

Silhouette Intimate Moments

Enter a world of excitement, of romance
heightened by suspense, adventure and the
passions every woman dreams of. Let us
sweep you away.

4 titles
per month

COMING NEXT MONTH

#652 THE ENCHANTED SUMMER—Victoria Glenn
When Derek Randall was sent to Green Meadow to buy the rights to the "Baby Katy" doll, he found himself more interested in rights holder Katy Kruger—a real live doll herself!

**#653 AGELESS PASSION, TIMELESS LOVE—
Phyllis Halldorson**
CEO Courtney Forrester had always discouraged office romances at his plant. But Assistant Personnel Manager Kirsten Anderson was proof that rules were meant to be broken....

#654 HIS KIND OF WOMAN—Pat Tracy
As the widow of his boyhood rival, Grace Banner was certainly not Matthew Hollister's kind of woman...until a passionate battle led Matthew to a tender change of heart.

#655 TREASURE HUNTERS—Val Whisenand
When Lori Kendall became a contestant on a TV game show she discovered that the only prize worth winning was teammate Jason Daniels. But would Jason's secret send Lori home empty-handed?

#656 IT TAKES TWO—Joan Smith
As concierge of an upscale Montreal hotel, Jennie Longman was used to catering to her guests' eccentric whims. But Wes Adler had a request that wasn't in Jennie's handbook. He wanted her!

#657 TEACH ME—Stella Bagwell
When secretary Bernadette Baxter started teaching her boss, Nicholas Atwood, the fine art of dating, she was soon wishing she was the woman who'd reap the benefits of her lessons....

AVAILABLE THIS MONTH

#646 A MATTER OF PRIDE
Sondra Stanford

#647 THE MEDICINE MAN
Melodie Adams

#648 ROSES HAVE THORNS
Karen Leabo

#649 STARRY NIGHTS
Wynn Williams

#650 LOVING JENNY
Theresa Weir

**#651 SILVER CREEK
CHALLENGE**
Amanda Lee